Great Writers & Kids Write Spooky Stories

Great Writers & Kids Write Spooky Stories

Edited by

Martin H. Greenberg, Jill M. Morgan, and Robert Weinberg

with illustrations by
Gahan Wilson

Random House 🏠 New York

Special thanks to:

Random House editor: Alice Alfonsi.

Random House book designer: Robert W. Kosturko.

*Additional thanks to Don Maass and the Don Maass Literary Agency;
and to Kate Klimo, Linda Hayward, Cathy Goldsmith,
and Jacqueline Dwyer of Random House.*

Photo credits: Beth Gwinn, p.10; Jenn Wilson, p.14; Sara Brooks, p.31; Karen Lansdale, p.50; Andrea Jakes, p.66; John Morgan, p.82; Richard Hill, p.96; John O'Callaghan, p.109; Susan Straub, p.122; Ann Costello, p.150; Erin Massie, p.165; Steve Rasnic Tem, p.180; Bonnie Hautala, p.192; David Stemple, p.207.

Library of Congress Cataloging-in-Publication Data:
Great writers and kids write spooky stories.
   p. cm.
Contents: What makes a story spooky? / Jill M. Morgan and Robert Weinberg — Introduction / Gahan Wilson — The maze / Ramsey, Tammy, and Matt Campbell — Closet monsters / Matthew J. and Nora Claire Costello — Abduction / Rick, Jesse, and Matti Hautala — Witch house / John Jakes and Jonathan Jakes-Schauer — The companion / Joe R., Keith, and Kasey Jo Lansdale — The merry music of madness / Elizabeth and Brian Massie — Zeus: the howling / Anne McCaffrey and Georgeanne Kennedy — Death and dagger / Jill M. and Terry A. Morgan — Wuffs / Maxine O'Callaghan and Brandon Apperson — In transit / Peter and Benjamin Straub — House full of hearts / Melanie and Joseph R. Tem — Itsy-Bitsy spider / F. Paul and Meggan C. Wilson — Daffodils / Jane Yolen and Heidi Elisabet Yolen Stemple.
ISBN: 0-679-87662-6 (trade) — ISBN: 0-679-97662-0 (lib. bdg.)
1. Horror tales, American. 2. Children's stories, American.
3. Children's writings, American. [1. Horror stories. 2. Short stories.
3. Children's writings.]
PZ5.G6977 1995
[Fic]—dc20
95-8583
Manufactured in the United States of America 10 9 8 7 6 5 4 3 2 1

WHAT MAKES A STORY SPOOKY?

by Jill M. Morgan and Robert Weinberg

It was a dark and stormy night...

Doesn't that sound like the beginning of a spooky story? Why? Because we can't see what's hidden in the *dark*.

There's even more that might be lurking in the *stormy night,* behind the roaring wind and blinding rain—until a bolt of jagged lightning streaks across the sky and shows us a face pressed against the window, or a ghostly figure standing beside us, reaching out...

One thing that good spooky stories have in common is *the unknown.* That's what scares us. Our imaginations try to picture what *might* be inside that abandoned house, within that dark room, or behind that closet door.

Would we be afraid of entering a well-lighted room, where we could easily see that the oddly shaped shadows were simply furniture? Probably not.

But that same room becomes a fearful place when the lights mysteriously fail. The familiar chest of drawers becomes a tall, bulky, threatening figure. The table lamp and nightstand change into the head, skinny neck, and four scrawny legs of some misshapen creature. A pillow and some discarded clothes are just part of a messy room when the lights are on. Turn off the lights, and they become a creepy scarecrow, a ghost, or *something* that slithered out of the closet.

Some of the best scary stories don't have ghosts or monsters. Instead, they have *dramatic tension*. The authors create moments in the stories where the readers hold their breath. The door blows open, an icy wind rushes into the room, an eerie, inhuman cry breaks the silence, and then…That's where authors want to take readers, to a place where tension quickens our pulses and grabs our attention.

There is something else a good spooky story often has. The element of *surprise*.

Whether it's a door slamming, the unexpected sound of a raspy breath right beside us, or a cliff top that abruptly crumbles beneath our feet, *surprise* is the crash that startles us. "Oh!" we say. "We didn't know *that* was going to happen!"

The spooky stories in this anthology are crafted using all three ingredients: the unknown, dramatic tension, and surprise. Look for these as you read through the collection.

A good spooky story does one more thing, too. It tells us something about ourselves. Most of us fear something. And most of us love a good scare.

What is hidden in the darkness of *your* room? What is lurking behind *your* closet door? What are *you* afraid of?

The answers might surprise you—and give you some ideas for writing your own spooky stories!

CONTENTS

Introduction
by Gahan Wilson

ITSY-BITSY SPIDER
F. Paul Wilson and adult daughter Meggan C. Wilson

ZEUS: THE HOWLING
Anne McCaffrey and adult daughter Georgeanne Kennedy

THE COMPANION
Joe R. Lansdale, son Keith Lansdale (age 12),
and daughter Kasey Jo Lansdale (age 8)

WITCH HOUSE
John Jakes and grandson Jonathan Jakes-Schauer (age 12)

DEATH AND DAGGER
Jill M. Morgan and adult son Terry A. Morgan

THE MAZE
Ramsey Campbell, daughter Tammy Campbell (age 16),
and son Matt Campbell (age 13)

INTRODUCTION

by Gahan Wilson

It is interesting that the majority of these stories, about the strange and sometimes terrible, have used children's bedrooms as the vortex of their adventures. It is especially interesting to find it so in a collection of tales that have been partially written and approved of by children themselves.

There are many good reasons for this. Perhaps the most outstanding is that a young child's bedroom is the first and only place in the whole world where adults officially allow a child to be entirely alone. It is in this room that children must undergo their first experience of separation. It is here that they begin to fumble with the thousands of challenges associated with being on their own.

The bedroom is also where children dream. In dreams, children wander farther yet from parental comforting. There are no adults to reassure them that the world is a solid, safe, and sensible place.

Still I find myself suffused with an oddly warm glow when I think of the bedrooms of my childhood. I remember the way an alley in Evanston looked on a gray twilight in fall; how it took me a week's worth of secret naptime scribbling to draw the grinning face of a black-patched pirate over two blank end pages in a picture book; or how a mother guppy dropped countless squirming babies before my bulging eyes and then, by heaven, ate them!

I had encounters with ghosts in two of those bedrooms. One was in a house in Old Lyme, Connecticut, a lovely old colonial job seated with great dignity hard by a salt marsh. I was very, very young, and I remember lying in bed and gazing raptly at the thick clumps of marsh mist floating in and out of the windows. I watched in wonder as they took on all sorts of marvelous and fantastic shapes.

Then, as though I'd heard some sort of signal, I sat up and wiggled my way to the foot of the bed. Leaning against the bed's footboard, I peered out the bedroom door and across the hallway to the steps that led up to the attic.

There, at the top of the stairway, was a tall glowing thing. I stared at it for a long time, telling myself it was only more mist, but I knew that was not true. It did not waver. It did not float. It was—in its ectoplasmic way—solid.

I moved thoughtfully back to the head of the bed to consider the matter, and then returned to the footboard to take another look. When I saw that, while unwatched, the glowing thing had extended a leg-sized column of itself to the next step down, I very wisely returned to my pillow and went to sleep as soon as possible.

The other ghost was considerably grimmer. My parents took me with them to visit friends who had recently opened an upscale country restaurant—it was a quaint old eighteenth-century house, which was known far and wide as the Octagon House because the thing was an eight-sided wooden tower.

After dinner, however, I learned that the shape of the house was not the only unusual thing about the place. Our hosts told my mother and father over brandy, and me over milk and cookies, that the Octagon House was the site of a famous and unusually horrible kidnapping.

The husband and wife who had built the place made a serious mistake when they hired a strange old woman to look after their child. In spite of the woman's harmless, grandmotherly appearance, she turned out to be a lunatic who stole their little boy one dark and stormy night. I clearly recall that my jaw froze midbite on a tollhouse cookie as that revelation was followed by a great crash of thunder.

I was led upstairs immediately after that story—sometimes it's hard to *believe* grownups! I was put, all alone, in a high-ceilinged antique room, where I soon found my small body curled up on less than ten percent of a huge four-poster bed. The only thing that relieved the room's ominous darkness was the increasingly frequent flashing that signaled the approach of a truly spectacular thunderstorm.

All the "dark old house" clichés presented themselves in perfect order: the wind howled mournfully through the tall trees; their twiggy branches clawed at the windowpanes; a loose shutter banged loudly and angrily on the wall near my head; and ominous, suggestive creakings snaked along the wide floorboards.

Then I saw it.

At first just a glimpse of it emerged from a sort of alcove. There it was; then there it wasn't. A pale blur, a part of something *peeking*. There it was again, floating about five feet high, the likely height of a bowed old woman of the 1700s. Then it swayed back out of sight.

It made its brief showings craftily, between flashes of lightning. I could not see it clearly for all its stealthy comings and goings, but I *had* to know what it was. I knew this from some amazing depth within me that I had never plumbed before and have seldom plunged into since.

I moved to the edge of the bed and slid softly down its side. After my small bare feet rested on the carpet, I stood. The thing floated into sight teasingly once more. Now I knew for sure that the corpse-colored blur was exactly the right size and shape for an old woman's face.

I advanced on it, forcing every step. The thing continued to hover in place until I was almost nose to nose with its crumpled surface. *Then the lightning flashed again to reveal the hideously wrinkled, madly grinning face of an eyeless hag...*

And I realized it was only a shaggy washcloth swaying on a draft-blown, swinging rack.

Gahan Wilson

When Bob Weinberg and Jill Morgan contacted Paul about collaborating with one of his children on a story, he thought it was a great idea. Meggan was 22 at the time and already writing on her own. Paul had been helping her with a poem that she wanted to adapt to a children's book. Since the poem ("No Tarantulas, Please") derived from Meg's lifelong fear of spiders (eeeuuw!), they decided to center their story around that fear.

They discussed—but did not write down—an outline of the story and how it should progress. Paul came up with a situation that he thought would allow Meg to tap into her fears and infuse them into the story. Meg came up with the diabolical ending. Then Meg sat down and banged out the first half of the story in one day. Paul embellished that and carried it to its close. Then they tweaked and polished it until both were happy with the final form.

The working title was "Spiders," but neither writer was too keen on that. A browse through Bartlett's *Familiar Quotations* yielded a line about a "silken tent" from a Robert Frost poem that could be used to refer to giant webs—"In Silken Tents"…yeah…

Nah. Too highbrow for a story that's anything but. Better to remember the KISS rule—Keep It Simple, Stupid.

So here's "Itsy-Bitsy Spider"— from a dad who thinks spiders are cool, and a daughter who forced herself to see the movie *Arachnophobia* but kept her feet off the floor the whole time.

Paul the   Meggan C. Wilson

ITSY-BITSY SPIDER

by F. Paul Wilson and Meggan C. Wilson

The moon was high before Toby spotted the first one—a hairy hunter. The hunters came out only at night. He hadn't seen this one before.

It was big, but not thick and bulky like a tarantula. This one's sleek body was the size of a German shepherd's. Its eight long, powerful legs were spread half a dozen feet on either side, carrying its head and abdomen low to the ground. Moonlight gleamed off its short, bristly fur as it darted across the backyard, seeming to flow rather than run. Hunting, hunting, always hungry, always hunting.

A cool breeze began to blow through the two-inch opening of Toby's screened window. He shivered and narrowed it to less than an inch, little more than a crack. It wasn't the air that was making him shiver. It was the spider. You'd think that after a year of watching them every night, he'd be used to them. No way.

Man, he hated spiders. Had hated them for the entire ten years of his life. Even when they were tiny and he could squash them under his foot, they had made his skin crawl. Now, when they were as big as dogs—even though there were no more dogs because the spiders had eaten them all, along with the cats and squirrels and woodchucks and just about anything else edible, including people—

the sight of them made Toby almost physically ill with revulsion.

And yet still he came to the window and watched. A habit—like tuning in to a bad sitcom—it had become a part of his nightly routine.

He hadn't seen this one before. Usually the same spiders traveled the same routes every night at about the same time. This one could be lost, or maybe it was moving in on the other spiders' territory.

It darted to the far side of the yard and stopped at the swing set, touching the dented slide with a foreleg. Then it turned and came toward the house, passing out of Toby's line of sight. Quickly he reached out and pushed down on the window frame until it clicked shut. The spider couldn't get in, Toby knew, but not being able to see it made him nervous.

He clicked on his flashlight and flipped through his spider book until he found one that looked like the newcomer. He'd spotted all kinds of giant spiders in the last year—black widows, brown recluses, trap-door spiders, jumping spiders, crab spiders. Here it was: Lycosidae—a wolf spider, the most ferocious of the hunting spiders.

Toby glanced up and stifled a scream. There, not two feet away, hovering on the far side of the glass, was the wolf spider. Its hairy face stared at him with eight eyes that gleamed like black diamonds. Toby wanted to run shrieking from the room, but he couldn't move—didn't *dare* move.

It probably didn't see him, didn't know he was there. The sound of the window closing must have drawn it over. Sudden motion

might make it bang against the glass, maybe break it, let it in. So Toby sat frozen and stared back at its cold black eyes, watched it score the glass with the claws of its poisonous falces. He had never been this close to one before. He could make out every repulsive feature. Every fang, every eye, every hair was magnified in the moonlight.

Finally, after what seemed an eternity, the wolf spider moved off. Toby could breathe again. His heart was still pounding as he wiped the sweat from his forehead.

Good thing they don't know glass is breakable, he thought, *or we'd all be dead.*

They never tried to break through anything. They preferred to look for a passage—an open window, an open door...

Door! Toby stiffened as a sudden chill swept over him. The back door to the garage—had he closed it all the way? He'd run some garbage out to the ditch in the back this afternoon, then he'd rushed back in. He was terrified of being outside. But had he pulled the door all the way closed? It stuck sometimes and didn't latch. A spider might lean against it and push it open. It still couldn't get into the house, but the first person to open the door from the laundry room to the garage—

He shuddered. That's what had happened to the Hansens, who'd lived down the street. A spider had gotten in, wrapped them all up in a web, then laid a huge egg mass. The baby spiders hatched and went to work. When the searchers finally found the family's remains, they looked like mummies and their corpses weighed only a few pounds each. Every drop of juice had been sucked out of them.

The garage door...maybe he'd better check it again.

"Don't be silly," he mumbled to himself. "Of course I latched it. I've been doing the same thing for almost a year now."

Toby left the window and brushed his teeth. He tiptoed past his mother's bedroom and paused. He heard her steady slow breathing and knew she was fast asleep. She was an early riser...didn't have much to stay up late for. Toby knew she missed Dad, even more than he did.

Dad had volunteered for a spider kill-team. "Doing my civic duty," he'd said. He never came back from one of the search-and-destroy missions. That had been seven months ago. No one in that kill-team had ever been found.

Feeling very alone in the world, Toby padded down the hall to his own room where even thoughts of monster spiders couldn't keep him from sleep. He had a fleeting thought of the garage door—yes, he was sure he'd latched it. Then his head hit the pillow, and he was instantly asleep.

Toby opened his eyes. Morning. Sunlight poured through the windows. A year or so ago it would be a day to go out and play. Or go to school. He'd never thought that he'd miss school, but he did. Mostly he missed other kids. The spiders had made him a prisoner of his house, even in the daytime.

He dressed and went downstairs. He found his mother sitting in the kitchen, having a cup of instant coffee. She looked up when she saw him come in.

"Morning, Tobe," she said, and reached out to ruffle his hair.

Mom looked old and tired, even though she was only thirty-two. She was wearing her robe. She wore it a lot. Some days she never got out of it. What for? She wasn't going out, no one was coming to visit, and she'd given up on Dad's coming home.

"Hey, Mom," he said. "You should have seen them last night— the spiders, I mean. One crawled right up to the window. It was real scary; like it was looking right at me."

Fear flashed in her eyes. "It came up to the window? That worries me. Maybe you shouldn't sit by that window. It might be dangerous."

"C'mon, Mom. I keep the window shut. It's not like I have anything else to do. Besides, it can't break through the glass, right?"

"Probably not. But just play it safe, and move away if one seems to be coming near you, okay? I don't know how you can stand to even look at those things." She grimaced and shivered.

Toby shrugged and poured himself some cereal. They were running low on powdered milk, so he ate it dry. Dad had stocked the whole basement with canned and freeze-dried food before he left, but those wouldn't last forever.

When he finished eating, he turned on the TV, hoping there'd be some news about a breakthrough against the spiders. The cable had gone out three months ago. News shows and *I Love Lucy* re-runs were the only things playing on the one channel that they could pull in with the antenna.

At least they still had electricity. Although the telephone worked only when it felt like it, the power lines were underground.

Those people whose power came in on utility poles weren't so fortunate. The spiders strung their webs from the lines and eventually shorted them all out.

No good news on the tube—just a rehash about the coming of the spiders. Toby had heard it all before, but he listened again anyway.

The spiders. No one knew where they came from, or how they became so big. Toby had first heard of them on the evening news about a year and a half ago. Reports came in from the Midwest, the farmlands, of cattle being killed, mutilated, and eaten. Then whole families began disappearing, their isolated houses found empty of life and full of silky webs.

It wasn't long before the first giant spiders were spotted. Just horrid curiosities at first, science fiction beasties. Local governments made efforts to capture and control them. Hunting parties went out with shotguns and high-powered rifles to "bag a big one." But these weren't harmless deer or squirrels or pheasants. These things could fight back. Lots of mighty hunters never returned. Toby wondered if the spiders kept hunters' heads in their webs as trophies.

The army and the National Guard got involved. For a while it looked as though they were winning, but the spiders multiplied too fast. They laid a couple thousand eggs at once; each hatchling was the size of a gerbil, hungry, and growing all the time. Soon they were everywhere—overrunning the towns, infesting the cities. And now they ruled the night. The hunting spiders were so fast and so deadly, no one left home after dark anymore.

But people could still get around during the day—as long as they stayed away from the webs. The webbers were fat and shiny and slower; they stretched their silky nets across streets and alleys, between trees and bushes—and waited. They could be controlled... sort of. Spider kill-teams could fry them with flamethrowers and destroy their webs, but it was a losing battle: the next day there'd be a new web and a new fat, shiny spider waiting to pounce.

And sometimes the spiders got the kill-teams...like Dad's.

Toby didn't like to think about what probably happened to Dad, so he tuned the TV to its only useful purpose: Sega. NHL Hockey and Mortal Kombat II were his favorites. They helped keep him from thinking too much. He didn't mind spending the whole day with them.

Not that he ever got to do that. Mom eventually stepped in and made him read or do something "more productive" with his time. Toby couldn't think of anything more productive than figuring out all of the Mortal Kombat II warriors' secret weapons and mortalities, or practicing breaking the glass on NHL Hockey, but Mom just didn't get it.

Today he knew he'd get in some serious Sega. Mom was doing laundry. She'd just keep making trips up and down to the basement and wouldn't notice how long he had been playing.

As the computer bellowed out, "Finish him!" he heard a cry and a loud crashing sound. He dropped the controller and ran into the kitchen. The basement door was open. He looked down and saw his mother crumpled at the bottom of the steps.

"Mom!" he cried, running down the steps. "Mom, what happened? Are you okay?"

She nodded weakly and attempted to sit up, but groaned in agony and clutched at her thigh. "My leg! It's my leg."

Toby helped her lie down again. She looked up at him. Her eyes were glazed with pain.

"I tripped on the loose board in that step," she said, and pointed to the spot. "I think my leg is broken. See if you can help me get up."

Toby fought back tears. "Don't move, Mom."

He ran upstairs and dialed the number for Dr. Murphy, their family doctor, but the phone was out again. He pulled pillows and blankets from the linen closet and surrounded his mother with them, trying to make her as comfortable as possible.

"I'm going to get help," he said, ready for her reaction.

"Absolutely not. The spiders will get you. I lost your father. I don't want to lose you, too. You're not going anywhere, and I mean it." But her voice was weak. Toby thought she was going into shock.

Toby knew he had to act fast. He kissed her cheek and said, "I'm going for Doc Murphy. I'll be right back."

Before his mother could protest, he was on his way up the steps, heading for the garage. The Murphy house was only a few blocks away. He could bike there in five minutes. If Dr. Murphy wasn't in, Mrs. Murphy would know how to help him.

He could do it. It was still light out. All he had to do was steer clear of any webs and he'd be all right. The webbers didn't chase their prey. The really dangerous spiders, the hunters, came out only at night.

As his hand touched the handle of the door into the garage, he hesitated. The back door—he had closed it yesterday…hadn't he? Yes. Yes, he was sure. Almost positive.

Toby pressed his ear against the wood and flipped the switch that turned on the overhead lights in the garage, hoping to startle anything lying in wait on the other side. He listened for eight long legs rustling about…but heard nothing. It was quiet in there.

Still, he was afraid to open the door.

Then he heard his mother's moan from the basement and knew he was wasting time. *Have to move. Now or never.*

Taking a deep breath, he turned the handle and yanked the door open, ready to slam it closed again in an instant. Nothing. All quiet. Empty. Just the tools on the wall, the wheelbarrow in the corner, his bike by the back door, and the Jeep. No place for a spider to hide…except under the Jeep. Toby had a terrible feeling about the shadows under the Jeep. Something could be there…

Quickly he dropped to one knee and looked under it—nothing. He let out a breath he hadn't realized he was holding.

He closed the door behind him and headed for his bike. Toby wished he could drive. It'd be nothing to get to Doc Murphy's if he could take the Jeep. He checked the back door. Yeah, it was firmly latched. All that worry for nothing. He checked the backyard through the window in the door. *Nothing moving. No fresh webs.*

His heart began to pound against the inner surface of his ribs as he pulled the door open and stuck his head out. All clear. Still, anything could be lurking around the corner.

"I'm going for Doc Murphy. I'll be right back." It had sounded

so simple down in the basement. But now…

Gritting his teeth, he grabbed his bike, pulled it through the door, and hopped on. He made a wide swing across the grass to give him a view of the side of the garage. *No web, nothing lurking.*

Relieved, he pedaled onto the narrow concrete path and zipped out to the front of the house. The driveway was asphalt, the front yard was open, and the only web in sight was between the two cherry trees to his left in front of the Sullivans' house next door. Something big and black crouched among the leaves.

Luckily he wasn't going that way. He picked up speed and was just into his turn when the ground to his right at the end of the driveway moved. A circle of grass and dirt as big around as a manhole cover angled up, and a giant trap-door spider leaped out at him. Toby cried out and made a quick cut to his left. The spider's poisonous falces reached for him. He felt the breeze on his face as they just missed. One of them caught his rear wheel and he almost went over, almost lost control. But he managed to hang on to the handlebars and keep going, leaving the spider behind.

Toby sobbed with relief. Man, that had been close! From the street, he glanced back and saw the trap-door spider backing into its home, pulling the lid down over itself, moving fast, almost as if it were afraid. Toby started to yell at it, but the words clogged in his throat. A brown shape was moving across his front lawn, big and fast.

Toby heard himself cry, "No!"

It was the wolf spider from last night! It wasn't supposed to be out in the day. It was a night hunter. The only thing that could bring it out in the day was—

Hunger.

He saw it jump on the lid to the trap-door spider's lair and try to force its way in, but the cover was down to stay. Then it turned toward Toby and started after him.

Toby yelped with terror and drove his feet against the pedals. He was already pedaling for all he was worth down the middle of the empty street, but fear added new strength to his legs. The bike rocketed ahead.

But not far enough ahead. A glance back showed the wolf spider gaining, its eight legs a blur of speed as they carried it closer. Its poisonous falces were extended, reaching hungrily for him.

Toby groaned with fear. He put his head down and forced every ounce of strength into his pumping legs. When he chanced another quick look over his shoulder, the wolf spider was farther behind.

"Yes!" he whispered, for he had breath enough only for a whisper.

And then he noticed that the wolf spider had slowed to a stop.

I beat him!

But when he faced front again he saw why the wolf had stopped. A huge funnel web spanned the street just ahead of him. Toby cried out and hit the brakes, turned the wheel, swerved, slid, but it was too late. He slammed into the silky net and was swallowed up in the sticky strands.

Terror swallowed him as well. He panicked, feeling as if he were going to cry or throw up, or both. But he managed to get a grip, get back in control. He could get out of this. It was just a stupid spider web. All he had to do was break free of these threads. But the silky strands were as thick as twine, and as sticky as Krazy Glue. He couldn't break them, couldn't pull them off his skin, and the more he struggled, the more entangled he became.

He quickly exhausted himself and hung there limp and sweaty, sobbing for breath.

I have to get free! What about Mom? Who'll help her?

Worry for his mother spurred Toby to more frantic squirming, but that only made the silk tighten its hold even more. He began shouting for help. Someone had to hear him and help him out of this web!

And then a shadow fell over him. He looked up. Something was coming, but it wasn't help. The owner of the web was gliding down from the dark end of the funnel, high up in the tree—and, oh, man, she was big. And shiny black. Her abdomen was huge, almost too big for her eight long, spindly legs to carry. Her eyes, spots that gleamed blacker than the black of her head, were fixed on him. She leaped the last six feet and grasped him with her forelegs.

Toby screamed and shut his eyes, waiting for the poisonous falces to pierce him. *Please let it be quick!*

But instead of pain, he felt his body being lifted and turned, and turned again, and again. He was getting dizzy. He opened his eyes and saw that the spider was rolling him over and over with her spindly legs, like a lumberjack on a log, all the while spinning yards and yards of web from the tip of her abdomen. She was wrapping his body in a cocoon, yet leaving his head free. He struggled against the bonds, but it was useless—he might as well have been wrapped in steel.

And then she was dragging him upward, higher into the web, into the funnel. He passed the shriveled-up corpses of squirrels and birds, and even another spider much like herself, but smaller—her mate?

Near the top of the funnel, she spun more web and attached him to the wall. Then she moved off, leaving him hanging like a side of beef.

What is she doing? Isn't she going to kill me? Or is she saving me for later?

Toby's mind raced. *Yes. Save me for later.* As long as he was alive, there was hope. Her web was across a street, and there was a good chance that a kill-team would come along and clear it—kill her, free him. Yes. He still had a chance....

Movement to his right caught his eye. About a foot away, something else was hanging from the web wall, also wrapped in a thick coat of silk. Smaller than Toby—maybe the size of a full grocery bag. Whatever was inside was struggling to get out. Probably some poor dog or raccoon that was caught earlier.

"Don't worry, fella," Toby said. "When the kill-team gets me out, I'll see you get free too."

The struggle within the smaller cocoon became more frantic.

It must have heard my voice, he thought.

And then Toby saw a little break appear in the surface of the cocoon. Whatever was inside was chewing through! How was that possible? This stuff was as tough as—

And then Toby saw what was breaking through.

A spider. A fist-sized miniature of the one that had hung him here emerged. And then another, and another, until the little cocoon was engulfed in a squirming mass of baby spiders.

Toby gagged. That wasn't a cocoon. That was an egg mass. And they were hatching. He screamed, and that was the wrong thing to do because they immediately began swarming toward him, hundreds of them, thousands, flowing across the web wall, crawling up his body, burrowing into his cocoon, racing toward his face!

Toby screamed as he had never screamed in his life—

And woke up.

He blinked. He was paralyzed with fear, but as his eyes adjusted to the dawn light seeping through the window, he recognized his bedroom and began to relax.

A dream…but what a dream! The worst nightmare of his life! He was weak with relief. He wanted to cry, he wanted to—

"Toby!" He heard his mother's voice—she sounded scared. "Toby, are you all right?"

"Mom, what's wrong?"

"Thank God! I've been calling you for so long! A spider got into the house! I opened the door to the garage and it was there!"

The back door! he thought. *Oh, no! I* didn't *latch it!*

"It jumped on me, and I fainted," called his mother. "But it didn't kill me. It wrapped me up in a web and left. Come get me free!"

Toby went to leap out of bed, but he couldn't move. He looked down and saw that he wasn't under his blanket—he and his bed were webbed with a thick layer of sticky silk. He struggled, but after a few seconds he knew that he was trapped.

"Hurry up, Toby!" his mother cried. "There's something else in here with me all wrapped up in a web. And it's moving. I'm scared, Toby. Please get me out!"

Panicked, Toby scanned the room. He found the egg mass attached to his bedpost. A few inches from his head, it was wriggling and squirming with internal life, a many-legged horde of internal life.

We're going to end up like the Hansens!

"Oh, Mom!" he sobbed. "I'm sorry! I'm so *sorry!*"

And then the first wolf spider hatchling broke free of the egg mass and dropped onto his pillow.

Toby screamed as he had never screamed in his life.

But this time he wasn't dreaming.

Georgeanne: The reason I chose to collaborate on this story with my mother is really very simple: I was asked. Flattered I most definitely was, honored too. Terrified, completely! By asking me to collaborate with her, my mother provided me with a net—so to speak—that allowed me the freedom to err. If I fell, Mum's writing experience acted as my net, and she could deftly "catch" my errors or omissions. This collaboration has been an interesting and challenging experience for me, and I'm very pleased Mum asked me to write with her. Thanks, Mum. (She's completely cool, you know.)

Anne: I chose my daughter to collaborate with me on writing this tale because, even as a young girl in school here in Ireland, she had a knack of writing lurid horror stories. Since I was divorced, I often wondered what her teachers in Avoca-Kingston School thought of her home life if this is the sort of bent her mind took. Nevertheless, she was always getting very good marks in English and even took honors in her Leaving Certificate (the equivalent of a high school diploma). She used local stories from our Farriery Center in Shelton Farms, Arklow, when the Crying Child was a known manifestation in Kilbride. I made some suggestions, but it is more her yarn than mine.

ZEUS: THE HOWLING

by Anne McCaffrey and Georgeanne Kennedy

❁

My name is Zeus, and my parents say it proudly. I am a red Doberman pinscher.

Mom and Pop—my people—often tell visitors that I don't have many of the habits of my breed. I've rarely barked, and only growled when that was needed, but I've never *howled* at the moon before. So, of course, my mom and pop were surprised by what happened over those three nights.

I surprised myself.

Mom and Pop first moved here to Brookie Farm a few months back. Granted, it was far larger than our old place, but nonetheless it just wasn't *home* to me right away. It took me some time to get used to the new farm and all the sounds and smells of it.

I like familiar things. But here, the fields, trees, even the air were very different from the farm on which I was bred and reared. Frankly, I'm still getting used to the change.

I mean, I could recognize all the cars and lorries and stuff going by. We're right on the road here, and there are all kinds of new engine sounds and people sounds and noises and smells. First few days here, Mom said I drove her crazy, starting at every sound.

But I *never* howled.

By now I've got used to the sounds of the cars that are allowed to come into our yard. I've learned to ignore the others—unless they turn in. Then I'll growl a warning just in case the motor isn't someone Mom and Pop are expecting.

Like that day not long ago when I growled at all those heavy big cars driving by so slowly. I could have *walked* faster! Lots of cars, diesel and petrol, and a long black car with the smell of something else—no, not a smell, a feeling. It made me uncomfortable.

And then, of course, I had to get used to the cat Mom brought in. I was doing my very best to keep the rabbits and rats from the feed. I have to admit those little squirmy mice were harder for a big dog like me to catch. At least that's why Mom said she'd brought in this furry nuisance. I growled at the cat for the first couple of days until Mom spoke sharply.

"Now, Zeus, I'll have no more of that! Deek is here to stay and that's that. You're grand outdoors, but I simply won't have mouse droppings in my cupboards. So Deek's here to control that problem."

Well, I had to accept the firmness in her voice. So when Deek got old enough to listen instead of spit at me, we worked out a deal. I'd leave Deek alone if he kept the mice out of the house. But he wasn't to bother me when I went after rats outside.

That cat sure could move fast up the nearest tree, though. Kinda took the fun out of that game—especially after Pop got mad at me for chasing Deek up the telephone pole.

Eventually, Deek and I got to be reasonable friends. Suddenly, Deek was full grown, and it wasn't so smart anymore to chase him—not with those sharp hooks he'd grown at the end of his claws!

Now, on that morning—the same morning that I saw all of those *slow* cars rumbling by—Deek put on another of his vocal shows. He'd been very restless that day, in and out and in and out.

"Really, Deek," Mom said, "I don't know what's got into you, but you've been acting very strange."

I could have told her that. But, while Mom and Pop were very good to us, sometimes they'd get so busy with human things that they didn't always notice changes. I had, but Deek wasn't talking at me.

Mom opened the door and gently put Deek out. But he was back in before she could close the door.

"I thought you *wanted* out!" she said, exasperated, and tried to whoosh Deek out again.

I guess the wind was from the right quarter that morning, because I heard the sound. Mom did, too, though her hearing isn't anywhere as good as mine. I whined, telling her I'd noticed. Whining was not something I'd been known to do, so it signaled Mom that something was not right.

"What is it, Zeus?" Mom asked. "Is Deek getting on your nerves too?"

I whined in response and pressed closer to the door. Mom opened it fully, and Deek, ever quick, was back inside again. He began winding in between Mom's legs and tickling my nose with his tail.

His calls were now more urgent, demanding even, which a cat's oughtn't to be. But with the door now wide open, we were all able to hear the noise clearly.

"Something's hurt," Mom said, and kicked off her soft slippers. She put on her muddy old yard boots and her jacket.

Together, she and I—and Deek, weaving in front and behind us—crossed the farmyard. We walked beyond the little laneway and ventured into the forest that bordered our new farmland.

The sound we heard was most definitely eerie, and Deek was visibly upset.

"Well, Deek," said Mom, "that's a cat for sure, but I can't tell where. Lead on."

Mom was so silly sometimes—she honestly believed that a mere cat could understand what she was saying!

Of course, she might have meant for me to lead on, which was only sensible. I put my nose up and, sure enough, there was a *blood* smell on the breeze from the woods.

Giving my best impression of a bloodhound, I ventured off in the direction of the scent and the tortured cries. Almost happily, Deek bounded along by my side, keeping up with my trot. Show-off!

The forest was deep here, so we kept to the track toward the piteous cries. Beyond a thick stand of pines and wild shrubs, we came to a natural clearing. I had no trouble then finding the right shrub. A small striped cat was caught up in a terrible mess of wire. Mom gasped, startling the poor creature. It really was messed up: I could see the blood now where the snare had torn away the skin and flesh of one of her back legs as she had tried to free herself.

Now the cat was struggling to get away from the new menace of us. Her efforts only tightened the snare about her leg. I winced and ducked my head between my front legs at the thought of the pain she was causing herself. I once had caught a paw in a snare myself, but I'd had the good sense to bark loud enough for Pop to come rescue me.

Now, Mom is a very gentle human and ever so patient when she has a mind to be. Very slowly, she backed a step or two away from the trapped cat so as not to startle it into more writhings. She gave me the hand signal to sit and stay—I'm very good at hand signals. Seeing me settle, Deek sat, too. He didn't twitch so much as a whisker.

All the time making soothing sounds to the little cat, Mom got down on her hands and knees. When she saw the cat relax and stop pulling against the snare wire, she inched forward, almost as stealthily as I could. Gradually the cat got used to her, and then Mom was right by it. Slowly, she put out her hand. The striped cat tensed up, her eyes wild and her ears flat back. But Mom had a kindness about her that always helped calm the other farm animals.

The cat didn't move.

"Oh, you're a very brave fur person," Mom said, her voice soft and reassuring as it was when she helped Pop with the calving cows. "Such a brave one to endure that wicked, wicked snare. Now, I'm just going to reach forward. See? My hand is nothing for you to fear. I'm trying to help you, and so are Zeus and Deek. They told me you were in trouble and brought me here to help. They'll tell you I'm all right. Now, there…"

While she talked so softly she had moved her hand closer to the cat's head and let her have a smell of it. Then, quick as a flash, she grabbed the cat by the scruff of the neck, holding it immobile.

"Oh, this wretched, wretched snare," she muttered as she used her free hand to unwind the snare from the bloody leg. Despite her firm hold—and I knew very well how firmly Mom could hold—the cat managed to howl and lash out with her front paws. "Oh, I'm so sorry to hurt you. It'll only be a moment, puss. I simply have to get you free. Ah, there."

The cat's frenzied writhings had loosened Mom's hold on the back of her neck. Still howling, the poor thing tried to run away. But her mangled leg wouldn't work, and the cat flopped over on the ground, spitting and hissing.

Quickly Mom scooped her into her arms, using her own jacket to bundle her. She was very careful not to touch the injured leg.

As soon as we got back home, Mom went into the small room next to the kitchen and shut the door on us. As if we would have hurt the poor thing! I sat down, and Deek sat beside me. After all, we *had* helped Mom find the cat.

When she came out, she went directly to the telephone.

"John, it's Jean O'Toole over at Brookie Farm. How are you? Fine, thank you. Look, someone's been using illegal snares again in the woods beside us. This time it's a young cat that got caught. Would you please come out right away and see what you can do? Its back leg is a terrible mess. Great. Thanks, John. See you soon."

Then Mom turned back and saw us sitting there. "Oh, you are dears, aren't you! You're worried about the cat, too. But you'd best stay away from the door because I don't want the kitty upset any-more. John'll come fix her." Mom gave me one of her stern looks. "And you, Zeus, the smell of you alone probably has the poor thing losing a life or two."

Indignant at the insult, I looked around at my sleek dark red coat and muttered under my breath. "I don't smell!"

But John Greene did when he arrived—he always does, being a vet. He smelled, not only of cows, horses, sheep, and pigs, but of his own three dogs. I greeted him with a gentle nudge at his free hand—he had that big black case of his in the other, and it smells more than he does.

He gave me the usual pat on my head that I've come to expect from him. I think he likes me. I don't stare at him and, after the first couple of visits he made to Brookie, I don't even growl at his car.

"I've got her in the utility room, John," Mom said, and led the way, shutting me and Deek out again. But I got a quick glimpse of the little cat in my old puppy basket.

They spent a long time in there, but I stayed on guard, just in case. Then Pop came in and started making a sandwich. I went over to him, hoping something would fall to the ground or find its way into my mouth. Pop was always so hungry that nothing was ever left on his plate like there sometimes was on Mom's. Which she'd give to me.

"Hey, Zeus, lad," Pop said. "Where's everyone?"

Just then Mom popped her head out of the room and told him about rescuing the cat. And about Deek and me knowing the cat was in trouble and finding her for Mom.

"Hey, Zeus, you're a great dog," Pop said, giving my head a good stroke. I watched the sandwich, hoping for something to drop out of it. "I need your invaluable assistance when I've finished eating. You know those twenty calves in the long meadow? There's not a pick of grass left, so it's time we moved them across to the ten-acre field. Right?"

I gave him as disagreeable a look as I dared. I didn't want to go after all those daft calves again! Shucks, we just moved them into the long meadow! Besides, cows are even dumber than sheep.

"Now don't you be giving me any long-suffering looks, old Zeus. You're the best herder in the county, not to mention the smartest Dobie in canine history."

Buttering me up again, was he? Well, it worked. I couldn't resist praise. Especially when he meant it. So I rose to all fours, willing to take on the feisty, stupid young cattle if it meant pleasing him.

On our way to the long pasture Pop set out at a brisk walk, which was fine by me. Pop's always in a rush.

"Wonder what's going on at St. Bridget's?" Pop asked, looking farther down the road. There were a lot more cars than there usually were for whatever happens at that building. Parked on both sides of the road, too. "Well, I got the calves bunched near the gate, so it shouldn't take us long. We won't hold up traffic this time, will we, Zeus? Oh-ho, spoke too soon."

The daft calves had broken up into five smaller groups and had drifted far from the gate. Pop gave me the right look, and I set off to gather them into one group. Then we could move them as a herd up the road to the new pasture.

I quickly moved in on the first group.

Sheep, of course, were sometimes skittish, but they were easy enough to pester into moving where I wanted them to go. Cattle and their young were harder for me to handle because they had less respect for my size. And, let's face it, they were just plain dumb. The trick was to pretend to nip at their heels to scare them in the direction I wanted them to go. I had to be quick and clever when I darted in to nip or I'd get a knock up against the side of my head from one of those cloven hooves of theirs.

While I worked them up into one tight herd, I was aware of traffic on the road. I was hoping that all those cars would be gone before we had to take the calves out onto the road. Nothing I hated more than a car honking at me as if I really could make either sheep or cattle let the smelly metal things through. Herds and flocks, even single horses, had the right of way. No one in a car seemed to know that!

So, while I didn't take my time doing my job, I didn't hurry them—just distracted them so that the cars going by didn't spook them.

"Well, you timed that right, Zeus," Pop said approvingly as I mooched the herd up to the gate. "Everyone at the church has cleared off. Must have been a funeral."

Pop opened the gate. With one last look back at the church, he signaled for me to move the calves forward. As I trotted behind the beasts onto the road, I looked back, too, and saw a lone figure walking toward us.

The breeze brought a whiff of mothballs and a harsh acrid odor that Mom once told me came from drycleaning, whatever that was. I also caught the smell of onions, cabbage, and fry oil. These scents usually came from Old Joe Boyle, who lived in a cottage just beyond us, on the town side of Brookie.

When we were within throwing distance of the gate, wouldn't you know, one of those hairy rascals decided to break away.

"Zeus! Hold!" I held my position, keeping the main herd where they should be. Pop went *whooshing* with arms and voice, and the hairy little guy decided he was safer with his pals. So we ambled them down the road in their usual leisurely fashion because, of course, they had to try all the roadside weeds to find the tastiest. But they kept moving.

Pop moved ahead and opened the ten-acre field gate so they could see all the good green eats awaiting them. The first couple of cattle shifted into a trot, but the one wily guy decided to test me again. He wheeled about and started back the way we had just come.

But old Joe was there. He *whooshed* the calf good so it turned tail again and, mooing in alarm, trotted past all of his pals and tried to push his way to the front. Another balked just at the gate, so I gave him an intentional nip on his hock to remind him that he was onward bound! He bounded.

Pop closed the gate and patted me. "Good lad, Zeus."

He turned toward our visitor. "Morning, Joe. Thanks for the help."

"Ah, sure, Sam, and why not?" Joe smiled, tugging at his tie to loosen it. "Fine dog." And Joe, too, gave me a pat. Since he'd helped us, I decided to allow the familiarity.

"Who was all that for?" asked Pop, nodding back toward the church.

Old Joe's face stopped smiling. "Was a fierce tragedy, that was," he said, shaking his head. "I've never known a family to have such dreadful luck. You might think they'd been cursed er somethin'."

Well, I knew what *cursing* was—it was what bad men did a lot of. But families?

"Really?" asked Pop. He has a way of getting people to talk.

"Really," Joe agreed, still shaking his head. He took out a cloth and blew his nose into it real loud. "They only got through burying their four-year-old babe after a bout of fever took her. Now, just two years on, and the whole lot of them was murdered by a drunken driver. Near as well plowed them all into the ground in that little runabout they had, and he in some blasted foreign monster of a motor. A disgrace it was!"

"Indeed," Pop agreed, nodding first and then shaking his head in sympathy.

"Yep," Joe went on. "They buried their wee bairn at St. Patrick's, over in the old churchyard. But their kin have taken the rest of 'em to the new one by the crossroads. No space left by their wee daughter."

"Oh." Pop's tone had a touch of surprise to it.

"I think 'tis an awful shame that they've left the poor bairn so far away from the rest of her family."

"Really?"

Joe gave his head a stern shake. "Not right, you know. Families should lie together to await the Golden Trump."

"It's a nice sentiment," Pop said in his sort of buck-up tone.

"I got them kin of hers to leave a bouquet on her grave. There was so many flowers for everyone, it was only right to leave her some on the day."

"Poor wee mite," Pop agreed. "Well, thanks for your timely help, Joe." We'd reached our lane now, so we could leave Joe to continue on his own way home.

"Poor lonely wee mite," Joe added. Still shaking his head and leaving behind the odd reek of his clothes, he walked on down the road to his cottage beyond the bend. "Neither kith nor kin to solace her."

I followed Pop up our lane, wondering what sort of surprise Mom might have put out for my dinner.

I was terribly uncomfortable in my bed that night. I felt this fierce itch, and I licked the spots and scratched them, but nothing gave me much relief. I got up and circled about long enough to discourage whatever might be in the bedding. But in no position could I find ease.

Something was not right.

I got up and checked that my dinner bowl was clean—again. Deek wasn't in his usual nighttime curl on the shelf. I drank some water to give me something to do. Maybe I was thirsty.

But that wasn't it. Something was still not right, and it wasn't thirst that bothered me. I sniffed the air. Could the fox be prowling about our henhouse? But there wasn't a trace of fox scent.

I went into the front room to peer out at the road. Was someone walking home from the pub? The moon was just coming up over the trees. A dog howled, lonely, miserable. I shivered.

I knew the sound of that howl. It came from the dog on the next farm over. He was always making noise late at night when his master came home. But this wasn't his usual howl. He usually just complained. This was a sad, mournful, uneasy sort of howl.

As uneasy as I was feeling, though, I wouldn't go so far as to *howl.* I have my pride, you realize.

A shiver took me all down my backbone, right to my tail. Or what was left of it. Then, without even knowing at first that I was doing it, a low, slow rumble came out of my throat and ended up in a howly growl.

I nearly choked. Where did that come from?

The neighbor's dog heard me and answered. Without any self-control, I was howling right along with him!

I caught myself midnote and snapped my jaws shut. I couldn't believe that I had made such a noise. And in the *house.*

Of course, my unusual crying woke both Mom and Pop. They came down the stairs from their bedroom, fussing.

"What is it, old guy? What's wrong, Zeus?"

I sure couldn't tell them, since I didn't know myself. But the urge to howl came over me again, so I thought I'd better go outside. I was so upset that I whined, hoping to hurry them up to open the door for me. I even lifted a paw to scratch at the doorframe. I felt a strange urgency—an urgency I could barely understand.

My baffled people let me out.

"I wonder what it is. Old Zeus rarely takes on so," Mom said as I flew from the top step to the ground and took off.

I had no idea why I turned left, taking the shortest route to where I *had* to go. I flew over the five-barred gate into the home field and only had enough sense to stick to the headland.

The recently plowed ground was wet and would be hard to make speed over. In no time, I was at the far end of that field, and I heard other dogs howling up ahead of me. It was that same mournful, sad, lonely howl that bubbled up out of my throat again.

I cut it off midway so I could jump the hedgerow at the bottom of the plowed field. Across the long pasture I streaked, aware that I was *not* the only animal answering this strange summons.

There was a high wall separating our property from the church graveyard, but it didn't slow me. I leaped to the top and paused. It was true. I wasn't the only one to answer this weird call.

Somehow the neighbor's dog had got loose. He was there along with four other dogs, whom I didn't know, plus a scrawny old cat. They were sitting on a grave with a spray of white flowers that shone like a long tear in the moonlight. Then Deek crept in from the shadows, crying as piteously as the little trapped cat had that morning.

I joined them. I had to. I was compelled to.

The grave was small. When I got to it, I saw that the white flowers almost covered it. Deek rested one paw on it. I sat beside him, although there was not much room at the graveside right now, so

small it was, with all of us around it.

The dogs and the scrawny old cat who had been caterwauling louder than Deek all stopped their noise. Through the ground, the wail came.

I'd never heard a noise like it—slow, low, bereft of hope. My hackles rose instantly, and not even the shiver that went down my spine smoothed them. All of us raised our heads and howled. As soon as we stopped, the child's cry urged us to another effort.

We howled our hearts out, crying the tears the child could no longer shed. We stayed all night. At least the moon was down when Mom and Pop came looking for me. Other owners—no more happy with our howling than my people—arrived in cars to break up our mournful circle. Yet when they got there, they didn't break us up.

They saw the flowers. They saw us around the grave. I don't think any of them—even Mom and Pop, who are sensitive people where animals are concerned—heard the baby's wail. They should have, but they didn't.

Humans don't hear as much as they think they can.

For whatever reasons, though, they let us be and went home to get what sleep they could.

When the sky started to brighten, we were released. Deek and I went home, and so did the others—more had arrived during our long vigil. Deek and I slept the entire day through, exhausted by an event we didn't understand though we had been helpless to throw off the compulsion.

❖ ❖ ❖

The next night, both Deek and I were called again. Deek made it first because I had a terrible time getting Mom or Pop to open the door for me to go on duty.

"Are you going to howl until I let you out, Zeus?" Pop complained when he finally trudged down the stairs. "You've never carried on like this. What's up at the cemetery anyway? No one's been buried there for a couple of years!"

I raced off as soon as the door was cracked open, and I heard Pop doing some of that cursing.

"Here, you, where do you think you're going?" he added, and I heard him make a dive after me. "Jean, that hurt cat's gone too!"

I didn't wait for the striped one, but it managed to hobble all the way to the churchyard. More had come to keep the vigil. Most howled all the time, which almost deadened the baby's awful wail. Almost, but not all the way. You could feel it through your paws and your haunches, coming up out of the ground.

We kept our vigil three nights, just as we were asked to.

Mom locked the injured kitten in the small room because she'd opened the worst of her snare wounds following us.

Then, the fourth night, I got no call, no summons. Nor did Deek. I needed the sleep. I'd been no help to Pop for days.

The next evening, Mom and Pop put a leash on my throat. I had never had a leash on me before. I'd never needed one, being an obedient and well-trained dog. I reckoned I'd done something very, very wrong.

We walked down the road on that fine evening, right down to the churchyard—though it would have been much quicker the way

I *usually* went, across the fields.

They walked me right up to the spot where I had spent my nightly vigils. Only there was no more grave. Just raw wet dirt. To one side was a withered sheaf of flowers.

"You see, Zeus, it's all right now," Mom said, kneeling beside me and patting the ground at the very place where the wails had come up out of the ground at us. "She's with her folks now, in the new cemetery. Her kin knew that she needed to lie with her parents after all."

"You howled real good, Zeus. You did the trick," Pop added.

So I never had to apologize for howling. And I also never howled again. I never had such a good reason to.

Here's what we did. Before we wrote anything, we kicked our idea around until we understood the framework. We talked out the scenes, the character, the locale, and the kind of mood we wanted to establish. We wanted an old-fashioned scary campfire story. Something that once read could be told and retold; and if not told exactly right, would still succeed, if kept within the original framework.

Next, we outlined the story on paper. Dad sat at the machine, and Keith and Kasey sat next to him as we got started. We revised sentences, suggested sentences, and talked out scenes. After each scene was written, we read it aloud and discussed it, wrote and rewrote until we had it the way we wanted.

When it was finished, copies were made, and we each looked them over and made notes. Then we wrote a final draft.

Was it fun?

Most of the time.

There was a bit of unpleasantness. Sibling rivalry and a nervous dad, but in the end we made it.

Out of it came "The Companion."

We liked doing it enough, if the opportunity arose, we would do it again.

Joe R. Lansdale   Keith Lansdale

Kasey Jo Lansdale

THE COMPANION

by Joe R. Lansdale, Keith Lansdale, and Kasey Jo Lansdale

They weren't biting.

Harold sat on the bank with his fishing pole and watched the clear creek water turn dark as the sunlight faded. He knew he should pack up and go. This wonderful fishing spot he'd heard about was a dud, but the idea of going home without at least one fish for supper was not a happy one. He had spent a large part of the day before bragging to his friends about what a fisherman he was. He could hear them now, laughing and joking as he talked about the big one that got away.

And worse yet, he was out of bait.

He had used his little camp shovel to dig around the edge of the bank for worms. But he hadn't turned up so much as a grub or a doodlebug.

The best course of action, other than pack his gear on his bike and ride home, was to cross the bank. It was less wooded over there, and the ground might be softer. On the other side of the creek, through a thinning row of trees, he could see an old farm field. There were dried stalks of broken-down corn and tall dried weeds the plain brown color of a cardboard box.

Harold looked at his watch. He decided he had just enough time to find some bait and maybe catch one fish. He picked up his camp shovel and found a narrow place in the creek to leap across. After walking through the trees and out into the huge field, he noticed a large and odd-looking scarecrow on a post. Beyond the scarecrow, some stretch away, surrounded by saplings and weeds, he saw what had once been a fine two-story farmhouse. Now it was not much more than an abandoned shell of broken glass and aging lumber.

As Harold approached the scarecrow, he was even more taken with its unusual appearance. It was dressed in a stovepipe hat that was crunched and moth-eaten and leaned to one side. The body was constructed of hay, sticks, and vines, and the face was made of some sort of cloth, perhaps an old towsack. It was dressed in a once expensive evening jacket and pants. Its arms were outstretched on a pole, and poking out of its sleeves were fingers made of sticks.

From a distance, the eyes looked like empty sockets in a skull. When Harold stood close to the scarecrow, he was even more surprised to discover it had teeth. They were animal teeth, still in the jawbone, and someone had fitted them into the cloth face, giving the scarecrow a wolflike countenance. Dark feathers had somehow gotten caught between the teeth.

But the most peculiar thing of all was found at the center of the scarecrow. Its black jacket hung open, its chest was torn apart, and Harold could see inside. He was startled to discover that there was a rib cage, and fastened to it by a cord was a large faded valentine

heart. A long, thick stick was rammed directly through that heart.

The dirt beneath the scarecrow was soft, and Harold took his shovel and began to dig. As he did, he had a sensation of being watched. Then he saw a shadow, as if the scarecrow were nodding its head.

Harold glanced up and saw that the shadow was made by a large crow flying high overhead. The early rising moon had caught its shape and cast it on the ground. This gave Harold a sense of re-lief, but he realized that any plans to continue fishing were wasted. It was too late.

A grunting noise behind him caused him to jump up, leaving his camp shovel in the dirt. He grabbed at the first weapon he saw— the stick jammed through the scarecrow. He jerked it free and saw the source of the noise—a wild East Texas boar. A dangerous animal indeed.

It was a big one. Black and angry-looking, with eyes that caught the moonlight and burned back at him like coals. The beast's tusks shone like wet knives, and Harold knew those tusks could tear him apart as easily as he might rip wet construction paper with his hands.

The boar turned its head from side to side and snorted, taking in the boy's smell. Harold tried to maintain his ground. But then the moonlight shifted in the boar's eyes and made them seem even brighter than before. Harold panicked and began running toward the farmhouse.

He heard the boar running behind him. It sounded strange as it came, as if it were chasing him on padded feet. Harold reached the front door of the farmhouse and grabbed the door handle. In one swift motion, he swung inside and pushed it shut. The boar rammed the door, and the house rattled like dry bones.

The door had a bar lock, and Harold pushed it into place. He leaped back, holding the stick to use as a spear. The ramming continued for a moment, then everything went quiet.

Harold eased to a window and looked out. The boar was standing at the edge of the woods near where he had first seen it. The scarecrow was gone, and in its place there was only the post that had held it.

Harold was confused. How had the boar chased him to the house and returned to its original position so quickly? And what had happened to the scarecrow? Had the boar, thinking the scarecrow was a person, torn it from the post with its tusks?

The boar turned and disappeared into the woods. Harold decided to give the animal time to get far away. He checked his watch, then waited a few minutes. While he waited, he looked around.

The house was a wreck. There were overturned chairs, a table, and books. Near the fireplace, a hatchet was stuck in a large log. Everything was coated in dust and spider webs, and the stairs that twisted up to the second landing were shaky and rotten.

Harold was about to return to his fishing gear and head for the bike when he heard a scraping noise. He wheeled around for a look. The wind was moving a clutch of weeds, causing them to scrape against the window. Harold felt like a fool. Everything was scaring him.

Then the weeds moved from view and he discovered they weren't weeds at all. In fact, they looked like sticks...or fingers.

Hadn't the scarecrow had sticks for fingers?

That was ridiculous. Scarecrows didn't move on their own.

Then again, Harold thought as he looked out the window at the scarecrow's post, where was it?

The doorknob turned slowly. The door moved slightly, but the bar lock held. Harold could feel the hair on the back of his neck bristling. Goose bumps moved along his neck and shoulders.

The knob turned again.

Then something pushed hard against the door. Harder.

Harold dropped the stick and wrenched the hatchet from the log.

At the bottom of the door was a space about an inch wide, and the moonlight shining through the windows made it possible for him to see something scuttling there—sticks, long and flexible.

They poked through the crack at the bottom of the door, tapped loudly on the floor, and stretched, stretched, stretched far- ther into the room. A flat hand made of hay, vines, and sticks appeared. It began to ascend on the end of a knotty vine of an arm, wiggling its fingers as it rose. It climbed along the door, and Harold realized, to his horror and astonishment, that it was trying to reach the bar lock.

Harold stood frozen, watching the fingers push and free the latch.

Harold came unfrozen long enough to leap forward and chop down on the knotty elbow, striking it in two. The hand flopped to the floor and clutched so hard at the floorboards that it scratched large strips of wood from them. Then it was still.

But Harold had moved too late. The doorknob was turning again. Harold darted for the stairway, bolted up the staircase. Behind him came a scuttling sound. He was almost to the top of the stairs when the step beneath him gave way and his foot went through with a screech of nails and a crash of rotten lumber.

Harold let out a scream as something grabbed hold of the back of his coat collar. He jerked loose, tearing his jacket and losing the hatchet in the process. He tugged his foot free and crawled rapidly on hands and knees to the top of the stairs.

He struggled to his feet and raced down the corridor. Moonlight shone through a hall window and projected his shadow and that of his capering pursuer onto the wall. Then the creature sprang onto Harold's back, sending both of them tumbling to the floor.

They rolled and twisted down the hallway. Harold howled and clutched at the strong arm wrapped around his throat. As he turned over onto his back, he heard the crunching of sticks beneath him. The arm loosened its grip, and Harold was able to free himself. He scuttled along the floor like a cockroach, regained his footing, then darted through an open door and slammed it.

Out in the hall he heard it moving. Sticks crackled. Hay swished. The thing was coming after him.

Harold checked over his shoulder, trying to find something to jam against the door, or some place to hide. He saw another doorway and sprinted for that. It led to another hall, and down its length were a series of doors. Harold quickly entered the room at the far end and closed the door quietly. He fumbled for a lock, but there was none. He saw a bed and rolled under it, sliding up against the wall where it was darkest.

The moon was rising, and its light was inching under the bed. Dust particles swam in the moonlight. The ancient bed smelled musty and wet. Outside in the hall, Harold could hear the thing scooting along as if it were sweeping the floor. Scooting closer.

A door opened. Closed.

A little later another door opened and closed.

Then another.

Moments later he could hear it in the room next to his. He knew he should try to escape, but to where? He was trapped. If he tried to rush out the door, he was certain to run right into it. Shivering like a frightened kitten, he pushed himself farther up against the wall, as close as possible.

The bedroom door creaked open. The scarecrow shuffled into the room. Harold could hear it moving from one side to the other, pulling things from shelves, tossing them onto the floor, smashing glass, trying to find his hiding place.

Please, please, thought Harold, *don't look under the bed.*

Harold heard it brushing toward the door, then he heard the door open. *It's going to leave,* thought Harold. *It's going to leave!*

But it stopped. Then slowly turned and walked to the bed. Harold could see the scarecrow's straw-filled pants legs, its shapeless straw feet. Bits of hay floated down from the scarecrow, coasted under the bed and lay in the moonlight, just inches away.

Slowly the scarecrow bent down for a look. The shadow of its hat poked beneath the bed before its actual face. Harold couldn't stand to look. He felt as if he might scream. The beating of his heart seemed as loud as thunder.

It looked under the bed.

Harold, eyes closed, waited for it to grab him.

Seconds ticked by and nothing happened.

Harold snapped his eyes open to the sound of the door slamming.

It hadn't seen him.

The thick shadows closest to the wall had protected him. If it had been a few minutes later, the rising moonlight would have expanded under the bed and revealed him.

Harold lay there, trying to decide what to do. Strangely enough, he felt sleepy. He couldn't imagine how that could be, but finally he decided that a mind could only take so much terror before it needed relief—even if it was false relief. He closed his eyes and fell into a deep sleep.

When he awoke, he realized by the light in the room that it was near sunrise. He had slept for hours. He wondered if the scarecrow was still in the house, searching.

Building his nerve, Harold crawled from under the bed. He stretched his back and turned to look around the room. He was startled to see a skeleton dressed in rotting clothes and sitting in a chair at a desk.

Last night he had rolled beneath the bed so quickly that he hadn't even seen the skeleton. Harold noticed a bundle of yellow papers lying on the desk in front of it.

He picked up the papers, carried them to the window, and held them to the dawn's growing light. It was a kind of journal. Harold scanned the contents and was amazed.

The skeleton had been a man named John Benner. When Benner had died, he was sixty-five years old. At one time he had been a successful farmer. But when his wife died, he grew lonely— so lonely that he decided to create a companion.

Benner built it of cloth and hay and sticks. Made the mouth from the jawbone of a wolf. The rib cage he unearthed in one of his fields. He couldn't tell if the bones were human or animal. He'd never seen anything like them. He decided it was just the thing for his companion.

He even decided to give it a heart—one of the old valentine hearts his beloved wife had made him. He fastened the heart to the rib cage, closed up the chest with hay and sticks, dressed the scarecrow in his old evening clothes, and pinned an old stovepipe hat to its head. He kept the scarecrow in the house, placed it in chairs, set a plate before it at mealtimes, even talked to it.

And then one night it moved.

At first Benner was amazed and frightened, but in time he was delighted. Something about the combination of ingredients, the strange bones from the field, the wolf's jaw, the valentine heart, perhaps his own desires, had given it life.

The scarecrow never ate or slept, but it kept him company. It listened while he talked or read aloud. It sat with him at the supper table.

But come daylight, it ceased to move. It would find a place in the shadows—a dark corner or the inside of a cedar chest. There it would wait until the day faded and the night came.

In time, Benner became afraid. The scarecrow was a creature of the night, and it lost interest in his company. Once, when he asked it to sit down and listen to him read, it slapped the book from his hand and tossed him against the kitchen wall, knocking him unconscious.

A thing made of straw and bones, cloth and paper, Benner realized, was never meant to live, because it had no soul.

One day, while the scarecrow hid from daylight, Benner dragged it from its hiding place and pulled it outside. It began to writhe and fight him, but the scarecrow was too weak to do him damage. The sunlight made it smoke and crackle with flame.

Benner hauled it to the center of the field, raised it on a post, and secured it there by ramming a long staff through its chest and paper heart.

It ceased to twitch, smoke, or burn. The thing he created was now at rest. It was nothing more than a scarecrow.

The pages told Harold that even with the scarecrow controlled, Benner found he could not sleep at night. He let the farm go to ruin, became sad and miserable, even thought of freeing the scarecrow so that once again he might have a companion. But he didn't, and in time, sitting right here at his desk, perhaps after writing his journal, he died. Maybe of fear, or loneliness.

Astonished, Harold dropped the pages on the floor. The scarecrow had been imprisoned on that post for no telling how long.

From the condition of the farm, and Benner's body, Harold decided it had most likely been years. *Then I came along,* he thought, *and removed the staff from its heart and freed it.*

Daylight, thought Harold. In daylight the scarecrow would have to give up. It would have to hide. It would be weak then.

Harold glanced out the window. The thin rays of morning were growing longer and redder, and through the trees he could see the red ball of the sun lifting over the horizon.

Less than five minutes from now he would be safe. A sense of comfort flooded over him. He was going to beat this thing. He leaned against the glass, watching the sunrise.

A pane fell from the window and crashed onto the roof outside.

Uh-oh, thought Harold, looking toward the door.

He waited. Nothing happened. There were no sounds. The scarecrow had not heard. Harold sighed and turned to look out the window again.

Suddenly, the door burst open and slammed against the wall. As Harold wheeled around he saw a figure charging toward him, flapping its arms like the wings of a crow taking flight.

It pounced on him, smashed him against the window, breaking the remaining glass. Both went hurtling through the splintering window frame and fell onto the roof. They rolled together down the slope of the roof and onto the sandy ground.

It was a long drop—twelve feet or so. Harold fell on top of the scarecrow. It cushioned his fall, but he still landed hard enough to have the breath knocked out of him.

The scarecrow rolled him over, straddled him, pushed its hand tightly over Harold's face. The boy could smell the rotting hay and decaying sticks, feel the wooden fingers thrusting into his flesh. Its grip was growing tighter and tighter. He heard the scarecrow's wolf teeth snapping eagerly as it lowered its face to his.

Suddenly, there was a bone-chilling scream. At first Harold thought he was screaming, then he realized it was the scarecrow.

It leaped up and dashed away. Harold lifted his head for a look and saw a trail of smoke wisping around the corner of the house.

Harold found a heavy rock for a weapon, and forced himself to follow. The scarecrow was not in sight, but the side door of the house was partially open. Harold peeked through a window.

The scarecrow was violently flapping from one end of the room to the other, looking for shadows to hide in. But as the sun rose, its light melted the shadows away as fast as the scarecrow could find them.

Harold jerked the door open wide and let the sunlight in. He got a glimpse of the scarecrow as it snatched a thick curtain from a window, wrapped itself in it, and fell to the floor.

Harold spied a thick stick on the floor—it was the same one he had pulled from the scarecrow. He tossed aside the rock and picked up the stick. He used it to flip the curtain aside, exposing the thing to sunlight.

The scarecrow bellowed so loudly that Harold felt as if his bones and muscles would turn to jelly. It sprang from the floor, darted past him and out the door.

Feeling braver now that it was daylight and the scarecrow was weak, Harold chased after it. Ahead of him, the weeds in the field were parting and swishing like cards being shuffled. Floating above the weeds were thick twists of smoke.

Harold found the scarecrow on its knees, hugging its support post like a drowning man clinging to a floating log. Smoke coiled up from around the scarecrow's head and boiled out from under its coat sleeves and pant legs.

Harold poked the scarecrow with the stick. It fell on its back, and its arms flopped wide. Harold rammed the stick through its open chest, and through the valentine heart.

He lifted it from the ground easily with the stick. It weighed very little. He lifted it until its arms draped over the cross on the post. When it hung there, Harold made sure the stick was firmly through its chest and heart. Then he raced for his bike.

Sometimes even now, a year later, Harold thinks of his fishing gear and his camp shovel. But more often he thinks of the scarecrow. He wonders if it is still on its post. He wonders what would have happened if he had left it alone in the sunlight. Would that have been better? Would it have burned to ashes?

He wonders if another curious fisherman has been out there and removed the stick from its chest.

He hopes not.

He wonders if the scarecrow has a memory. It had tried to get Benner, but Benner had beat it, and Harold had beat it too. But what if someone else freed it and the scarecrow got him? Would it come after Harold too? Would it want to finish what it had started?

Was it possible, by some kind of supernatural instinct, for the

scarecrow to track him down? Could it travel by night? Sleep in cul-
verts and old barns and sheds, burying itself deep under dried
leaves to hide from the sun?

Could it be coming closer to his home while he slept?

He often dreamed of it coming. In his dreams, Harold could see
it gliding with the shadows, shuffling along, inching nearer and
nearer.

And what about those sounds he'd heard earlier tonight, outside
his bedroom window? Were they really what he had concluded—
dogs in the trash cans?

Had that shape he'd glimpsed at his window been the fleeting
shadow of a flying owl, or had it been—

Harold rose from bed, checked all the locks on the doors and
windows, listened to the wind blow around the house, and decided
not to go outside for a look.

—For Laura, Mi-Mi, and Mom

My oldest grandson and I collaborated on this story in the fullest sense. The concept, however, is Jonathan's. He says it came about this way:

> "I got the idea from a book of railway ghost stories. In one, a train comes alive and begins to eat people. I thought it would be interesting if a house came alive. After telling the idea to my grandfather, we sat down and stewed over it. That is where 'Witch House' came from."

When we "stewed over it," we discussed characters, plot points, and twists. I put everything down in a rough longhand outline. Most of the actual writing is mine, though Jonathan offered suggestions for revision, simplifying certain phrases in the final version.

There were no problems; the collaboration was a pleasure from beginning to end.

But I expected it to be that way. All eleven of my grandchildren are great kids. I just hope there are ten more anthologies, for ten more collaborations.

John Jakes · Jonathan Jakes-Schauer

WITCH HOUSE

by John Jakes and Jonathan Jakes-Schauer

✼

Joe discovered the old painting in the attic, two days after they moved in. The painting was turned to the wall, and covered with a dusty bedsheet.

He uncovered the picture and turned it around. He shivered. Then he felt embarrassed. Joe was twelve, big for his age, strong from a lot of soccer and baseball. Why should a picture of a middle-aged woman in funny clothes give him the creeps?

Maybe it was the eyes, pale as old bones. They stared right into his, full of hate.

The woman wore a long white apron over a dark dress. A white kerchief was tied around her neck; a loose-fitting hood framed her oval face. Her hands were folded at her waist. Time had cracked the artist's pigments, giving the painted flesh an eerie, scaly look.

Joe called down to his mother. She came up. Meg Adams was a tall willowy woman, good-looking but a little haggard. She was the sole support of the two of them.

She felt the spell of the portrait too. "I wonder if she lived here years ago? Poor woman, she looks so unhappy."

"Like she wants to hurt somebody," Joe said. "I mean, look at those eyes. They're really scary."

Meg brushed back a stray lock of her graying blond hair. "Then I suppose we shouldn't hang the picture downstairs." With an emphatic shake of his head, Joe agreed. "But I'm curious about her, Joey. Do you remember that small building off the square in town? It's the County Historical Society. Someone there might be able to tell us who she is."

"If you really want to know," Joe said, covering the portrait as fast as he could.

Getting settled in his new home, Joe forgot the painting for a few days. Joe's father, an attorney, had died suddenly the year before. Joe and his mother had moved to a new town where she found a job in a law firm. Meg was a skilled legal secretary.

The only house they could afford was many years old. Tall and roomy, it stood on an acre of ground, amid great live oaks hung with Spanish moss. Meg said it must have been repainted and repaired many times. Joe liked all the space, although Meg wondered why the rent was so low—probably the location, several miles from town, on a lonely dirt road. The nearest neighbor lived a mile away.

On a Thursday afternoon, Joe got off the school bus, waved, and headed for the house. It was late October, still warm and bright. He stood a moment on the wide front porch, enjoying the song of a mockingbird. A white egret sailed skyward from the salt marsh beyond the road.

With a sigh, he unlocked the front door. Mom wouldn't be home for at least two hours. He'd better start his homework. Otherwise, she would never let him watch a *Star Trek* rerun.

In his second-floor room, he turned his back on the sunlit windows and switched on his old, slow PC. Concentrating on a book report due the next day, he didn't notice the room growing darker. Suddenly, he heard a faint sound.

A woman, sobbing.

How could that be? There wasn't anyone else in the house. Was his mother home early? He went to the door and called, "Mom?"

The sobbing continued, one moment seeming to come from the attic, the next from downstairs. Joe's mouth was dry.

"Hello? Anybody there?"

The sobs grew louder, a strange echoing music of utter misery. Then Joe heard something else. He spun around. Rain was streaming down the windows—long, straight streaks of rain, like tears. Outside, the front yard was dark, sunless.

Scared though he was, he stepped into the hall and crept through the whole upstairs, room by room. Finding nothing, he went down the long, steep staircase and searched the ground floor, then the damp, gloomy basement. No one—just that sad sobbing. It was almost as if the whole house were *crying*.

He went to the front door, startled to see rain pouring down the panes of leaded glass. Impossible—*the porch sheltered the door with a six-foot overhang.*

Joe yanked open the door, expecting to be hit in the face with gusts of rain. He heard the mockingbird. The afternoon sun shone, just as it had when he'd stepped off the bus.

He ran into the yard, whirled, and stared up at the house. The windows of his room sparkled with slanting sunlight. They were dry. The roof was dry. The ground under his Reeboks was dry.

Am I crazy, or what?

After a minute, Joe took a deep breath, returned to the porch, and poked his head through the open doorway.

All quiet. The house had stopped its crying.

When Meg came home at six, Joe didn't tell her about the weird incident. He was afraid she'd think he was making it up. He even forgot to ask if he could watch the *Star Trek* rerun.

He had trouble falling asleep. Finally he did. He woke suddenly in the middle of the night, hearing a chilling sound.

Rain, running down the windows.

Somewhere, the ghostly woman began to cry. Joe lay rigid, cold sweat soaking his pajamas. He shut his eyes, clenched his fists. The crying went on, and on…

Somehow he fell asleep again. In the morning, at breakfast, his mom looked pale and anxious. As Meg sliced a banana for the corn-flakes she said, "I had a terrible nightmare during the storm." Joe's stomach flip-flopped. "I was listening to a woman moaning and weeping in the house, but I never saw her. You didn't hear anything odd, did you?"

Joe never lied to his mother, but he had to hedge now. "Don't think so."

At ten past seven they walked out of the house into a fresh, bright morning. Meg paused to study the Bermuda grass growing in the sandy soil of the lawn.

"The ground's perfectly dry. The storm must have lasted only a few minutes. I thought it went on for hours."

He could have told her there was something strange going on; probably *should* have told her. But he didn't want to scare her. And he wasn't quite sure he believed it himself. He fixed a smile on his face and answered with a shrug.

Meg hugged him and said good-bye. Soon her car disappeared down the road. Joe stood watching it grow smaller. He didn't look back at the house, not even when he boarded the school bus.

The brass plaque beside the door read:

COUNTY HISTORICAL SOCIETY
JUDGE ELI WOLVERTON (RET.), DIRECTOR

Joe knocked and stepped inside, out of the blustery weather.

"Yes, hello?" called a tall, spare man seated at a cluttered desk in a room off the hall. His face was tanned, his white hair cut short. He rose to greet his visitor. The office smelled pleasantly of old books, fine paper, and wood smoke from a grate where a cheery fire burned.

Joe took off his cap, then introduced himself. Judge Wolverton waved at an ornate wall clock showing ten past twelve.

"Shouldn't you be in school, young man?"

"I skipped lunch hour to talk to you, sir. It's important. My mother and I live in the old Lee house."

"Oh, you're the ones." The judge's face was less severe. "I'm sorry I haven't met you sooner. I was out West, visiting my son. I expect I know what's on your mind. Sit down."

Nervous in the presence of a former judge, Joe took a chair. He noticed a tall painting of a dignified black man in a frock coat, holding a law book. Across the hall, behind a glass exhibit case, a bearded officer in Confederate gray looked sternly down from a gilt frame.

"Something very strange happened at our house last week," Joe began.

"I'm not surprised. Tell me about it."

Joe did. At the end, the judge nodded. "That's Mary Lee, all right. The unfortunate woman in the painting you found. I thought that picture had disappeared long ago. Did you know the house stood empty for months before you and your mother rented it? The local real estate agents seldom show it to anyone."

"What's wrong with it?"

"It's too far from town, and that unpaved road's a fright. Also, the place has a reputation. They say the spirit of a witch lives there. An angry witch."

"But witches aren't real."

"The ignorant people who killed Mary Lee thought otherwise."

Judge Wolverton went on to say that in the year 1692, when fear of witchcraft was sweeping the American colonies, the woman named Mary Lee had been accused by her neighbors, and put to death.

"She was sixty-one years old at the time. A spinster—she never married. She lived all alone in the original house that her father built. She loved the place. A mob dragged her from it and hung her, not twenty steps from here. Standing on the gallows, she swore to get even for the injustice."

"Why did they think she was a witch?"

"They say Mary Lee cured the sick with herbal medicines, but she was secretive about the formulas and where she found the plants. Some would call that evidence of magical powers. If she did have such powers, there isn't one iota of evidence to prove she ever used them to harm others. Our only record of Mary Lee is right here."

From a locked case with its own temperature control, he took an oversized book with faded gilt lettering on the spine. He laid the book open in front of Joe. The inked handwriting on the yellowed page was so ornate, Joe couldn't read it. He did pick out the name Mary Lee.

"This is the only existing mention of the event—this one page from the township record for 1692. It states that Mary Lee was executed after a five-minute trial. It declares her an evil witch."

"You don't believe in such things, do you, sir?"

"Let me quote Shakespeare's *Hamlet*. 'There are more things in heaven and earth, Horatio, than are dreamt of in your philosophy.' It's a famous line. Also a pretty good answer to your question."

Joe stared at the page. Goose bumps prickled his arms. A burning log fell in the hearth; he almost jumped out of his chair.

"So Mary Lee causes trouble for whoever lives in her house?"

"Yes, but it happens only every sixty-one years—her age when she died." He penciled some figures on a pad. "There were incidents during the years 1753, 1814, 1875, and 1936." He looked at Joe with sympathy. "Now another sixty-one years have passed. You and your mother came along at a bad time."

Joe gulped. "What happened when she came back before?"

"The man who owned the house in 1814 died of a heart attack. He'd never been sick a day. In 1875, a freak fire killed two people. The 1936 tenants simply vanished one afternoon and were never seen again. We presume something similar happened back in 1753, but we have no record. If you believe the story, Mary Lee returns to her house every sixty-one years to make innocent people suffer, because she was innocent when her neighbors hanged her."

Joe thought of the hate-filled eyes in the portrait. He could understand why Mary Lee looked that way. Despite the bad things she'd done, he felt sorry for her, a woman without a husband or family. She was helpless against the fury of superstitious neighbors.

Judge Wolverton closed the book. "You be careful in that house, young man—you and your mother, too."

"We will," Joe promised. He thanked the judge. They shook hands, and the judge saw him to the door.

A dark November sky pressed down when Joe stepped off the bus later that afternoon. He unlocked the front door. No lights were on. Shutting the door, he heard snarling, as if a savage dog were about to attack. His heart raced.

"Mary Lee?" he called into the darkness. "I know about you. If you're here, I wish you'd leave us alone."

Wrong thing to say! The thought flashed through his head as he heard a crash from the living room. His mother's favorite print, big Monet water lilies, lay on the floor, its glass cracked. Meg had hung the print over the fireplace mantel. Now it rested in the archway entrance—*eight feet from the hearth.*

More crashes! In the dining room, dinner plates were jumping off the open shelves of a hutch, flying through the air like UFOs—smashing against the walls.

Joe raced in there. "Stop that—they're Mom's best dishes!" Another plate sailed toward his head. He ducked. The plate stopped in midair, reversed, flew the other way, and shattered against the wall. There was more noise in the kitchen. Joe shoved the swinging door open. "Oh, no!"

The refrigerator door sprang open. A plastic gallon of milk flew out, hovered while the blue cap popped off. The jug turned a somersault in the air. The milk poured onto the floor.

Then Meg's meat cleaver jumped from its hook and began to whack the chopping block below.

Kitchen drawers shot open. Silverware leaped out, flying toward the windows, shattering them like a hail of machine gun bullets. When the noise stopped, milk gurgled over the floor, deep scars marred the chopping block, silverware lay strewn in the Bermuda grass outside.

Joe heard the angry snarling change to a cackle of laughter that quickly faded away.

He was still cleaning up when Meg came home at five thirty. "What in heaven's name—? Joey, did someone break in?"

Joe dropped pieces of china into a paper grocery bag. "No, but someone's mad at me, because I found out about her."

"Who are you talking about?"

"The woman who lived here over three hundred years ago. The woman in that old picture. Mom, don't look at me like that. Sit down. I'll tell you what I know."

Shaking her head, Meg sank down on a kitchen chair. Joe patted her, put the tea kettle on, then repeated everything he'd heard from Judge Wolverton. He watched her face change as he spoke. Once she almost laughed, not believing what she heard. By the end, gazing at the sacks of broken china, she had a look of horror.

Joe set a steaming cup of herbal tea on the table beside her. Meg put her arm around him. "What are we going to do?"

"Call the sheriff?" he said, for want of any other idea.

"To do what? Arrest someone who isn't real?"

"She's real, Mom. I didn't believe it at first, but I do now. Maybe..." he said, hesitating. He blurted it out. "Maybe we should move."

Meg's face grew sad. "You know we couldn't find a place in town that we could afford. If we move, we'll have to leave, and I'll be lucky to find another job half as good."

"Then what can we do?" It wasn't often that Joe felt defeated, but he felt that way now.

Meg sipped tea, then squared her shoulders.

"I'll speak to her myself."

Panicky, he followed his mother through the dining room to the hall. At the foot of the stairs, she planted her fists on her hips.

"Listen to me, whoever you are. This house is ours, and I don't like what you're doing to it."

Outside, one of the decorative window shutters began to bang.

Joe's eyes bugged.

Other shutters began to bang. Meg was intent on calling to the spirit. "My son and I haven't hurt you—"

"Mom, shh! Don't make her mad again." Joe was sweating. The house was hot as an August afternoon when the air conditioning wasn't working.

"—if you come around tormenting innocent people, you're just as bad as the ones who sent you to the gallows. No, you're worse. You keep doing it!"

Every outside shutter was banging. Meg suddenly realized the temperature had shot up. "Joe, did you turn up the thermostat?"

He ran to the wall. "I didn't touch it. It's still set at sixty-eight."

But the house was boiling. *From Mary Lee's anger?*

"Stop this; it's cruel," Meg cried at the foot of the stairs. From the dark second floor came a growl of rage that made the walls shake. Joe felt the floor vibrate. Meg ran halfway up the stairs. "Who's there? Show yourself unless you're too cowardly."

"Mom, come down," Joe called, terrified. As his mother rushed on up the stairs, the walls and floor quaked, the shutters banged— then the staircase itself began to ripple like a rug being shaken.

Meg was thrown off the stairs by the wild undulations. She tumbled down with a cry that was suddenly cut off when she landed at Joe's feet, eyes closed, not moving. "Mom!" he screamed to her limp, twisted figure.

Judge Wolverton stood before the crackling fire. "I can't believe what I'm hearing. You're asking me to destroy what I'm paid to protect?" he asked Joe.

"So Mary Lee will stop."

Joe's voice was ragged. He was pale, with big circles under his eyes. He hadn't really slept last night, only dozed a few minutes on a hard bench in the hospital waiting room.

"How can you be sure it would do any good?" the judge asked.

"I'm not sure. I don't know about such things. I'm just trying. Something threw my mom down the stairs last night, and she's in the hospital—"

"With a bad concussion."

Joe nodded. "Doctor Mortimer said she's lucky to be alive. Sir, you told me the only thing saying Mary Lee was a witch was that one page." He pointed to the old book in the temperature-controlled case. "If it were gone, there'd be nothing at all. Maybe then Mary Lee would rest."

"My boy, you're asking too much. I am paid to care for the artifacts owned by this historical society."

"How many people have looked at that page this year?"

The judge thought a moment. "You're the only one. I haven't looked at it myself in over four years, and I only looked then to show a writer from New York who was researching a book on the occult."

"Judge, my mom almost died because of that one page."

"Oh, my boy, you exaggerate," the judge said in his best voice of authority. He faced the fire but turned back a moment later, studying the upset and exhausted boy.

"Stand aside," the judge said finally.

He strode to the window, glanced at the street where a few snowflakes whirled in the pale noon sunshine. Swiftly he drew down the blind. Next, he marched back to the special case, removed the old book, and opened it on his desk. He glanced from the page to Joe, and back again. He seemed undecided.

Then, taking a deep breath, he began to tear the page from the book. Joe watched it come away from the binding a bit at a time. Finally it was loose.

Judge Wolverton scanned the page. Then he tossed it on the fire.

The paper flared up with a soft explosive *whoosh*. There was a bad smell, as though a whole box of sulfur matches had ignited. The judge didn't look at the curls of ash. He kept his back turned, as if he couldn't bear to see what he'd done.

Doctor Mortimer released Meg after two days. There was no permanent damage. She and Joe left the hospital together. A dark green beret hid the bandage on Meg's head.

They took a taxi home. It was a bleak, rainy afternoon in early December. As they stepped out of the cab they smelled wood smoke.

"Joey, you didn't come home earlier and light a fire in the grate?" Meg asked as the taxi pulled away.

"Mom, I wouldn't do that."

She gripped his arm. "All the downstairs lights are on."

It was true. Every window showed bright yellow, a comforting glow in the December gloom. Joe said, "Everything was dark when

I locked up and left for school."

Meg's face was drained of color. Joe's heart was beating very fast as she unlocked the door.

In the hall, there was no sound except a soft pop of wood from the living room fireplace. In the archway, Meg put her gloved hand to her mouth. She stared at the portrait of Mary Lee hanging over the mantel.

"That picture was in the attic, Joey."

Bewildered, he said, "I didn't move it, I swear."

"Then who did?"

They looked at each other. The spot over the mantel had been empty ever since the water lily print fell. The print was in the front closet, waiting to go to the frame shop for new glass.

Joe stepped to the mantel. The back of his neck prickled. "Mom, look close. Something's different."

Mary Lee's pale eyes no longer glared with hate. They were gentle, ordinary. She looked like a pleasant, harmless old lady from long ago.

Somewhere a door closed. Meg jumped and threw her arms around her son.

But there was no danger, only a tinkling laugh, far away.

And then a faint voice, calling out to them:

"The house is yours. Good-bye, good-bye."

When they looked at the portrait again, Mary Lee was smiling.

The idea for "Death and Dagger" came about when Terry was about the age of the boys in the story. There is such a place in our town, dangerous and fascinating to kids determined to find an adventure. I heard about it long after Terry explored the tunnel, and I was horrified to imagine what might have happened if he'd become trapped there. That kind of fear stays with a parent.

The thought of turning Terry's experience into a short story always tempted me, but it was his story. I kept telling myself that. He kept telling me that. We waited. When the opportunity for us to write a story together came up, this was the obvious choice.

This isn't Terry's first collaboration. He has also co-written a screenplay with his brother Chris, as well as a short story titled "Zaambi." Terry also writes film review columns for the *Pasadena Weekly* and the *Capitola Courier*.

In writing this story together, I got to borrow from the event that haunted my mind as a parent, and he got to make it sound even spookier than it actually was. At least, I hope that's true. Maybe he hasn't told me everything about that day. I wonder. Maybe there really was *something* buried in that rat- and spider-infested tunnel....

DEATH AND DAGGER

by Jill M. Morgan and Terry A. Morgan

❀

The entrance to the abandoned tunnel was closed by a rusty iron grating. Painted on the grating was a skull and crossbones and the words STAY OUT.

Twelve-year-old Ben Donovan thought the crossbones looked like daggers, which he guessed was how the place got its name.

"Too bad we can't get in there," said Ben's friend Matt.

"Yeah," said his other friend Danny. "Imagine exploring all those tunnels."

"I found a way," said Ben. He had Danny's and Matt's complete attention.

"My dad says this whole flood channel's on an earthquake fault," said Danny.

"Your dad doesn't know everything," said Matt. "Show us what you found, Ben."

Ben walked along the track of dry riverbed. He stopped a few feet below a rise of rocks up ahead. "Over here," he called to them.

"Where?" asked Danny.

Ben pointed to a hole in the ground.

Matt and Danny stepped closer and peered into the hole. It was wide enough for a grown man to squeeze through the opening. But it was so dark, they couldn't see what was beneath the surface.

"How do we know what's down there?" asked Danny, taking a step back.

"Isn't that the idea?" Ben asked. "To find out?"

A sudden gust of wind blew dust from the riverbed around their feet, like a chill warning.

"You guys chicken?" asked Ben.

"No." Danny looked scared, but Ben knew he wouldn't run, not unless Matt chickened out too. There was a dead silence as both of them turned to look at Matt, waiting for what he'd say.

"Shine the light into the hole," said Matt.

Ben switched on the flashlight and pointed the beam into the opening in the ground. All three of them leaned over the edge and looked. Matt picked up a pebble and dropped it. A few seconds later the pebble struck bottom, pinging against the inside floor of the concrete pipe.

"Ten or twelve feet," said Ben. "Are we going, or aren't we?"

"Give me the flashlight," said Matt.

Ben gave it over.

"See ya," Matt said, and jumped.

Ben dropped to his knees, leaning as close as he dared to the opening in the ground. "Matt!" he called, trying to see into the dark.

"Jeez," said Danny. "He really did it."

"C'mon," Ben said, grabbing Danny by his shirtsleeve. He wasn't about to have Matt call *him* chicken. He jumped into the opening, hitting the concrete floor of the tunnel with a thud. A couple of seconds later, he heard Danny drop right beside him.

"Matt!" Ben called. It was too dark to see.

There was no answer. But as Ben moved forward, he began to make out something weird up ahead. It was dull, but glowing.

"Is that the flashlight?" asked Danny.

Ben wasn't sure.

"Are you guys coming, or what?" Matt's voice came from the same place as the light.

"Wait for us," called Ben, dragging Danny with him. They ran to catch up.

"Took you long enough," said Matt.

The tunnel was creepy. A layer of dried mud and some kind of slime coated the concrete floor. The place was so thick with spider webs that the flashlight beam was dulled by them, as if it were shining through thin layers of cotton.

They walked until Ben's foot kicked against something solid. He nearly tripped, saving himself at the last second from falling on his hands and knees into the slime. "Shine the flashlight over here," he told Matt.

A pile of rock and broken cement covered a wide space in the tunnel. "Looks like some kind of cave-in," said Matt.

Ben nudged a few of the rocks with the toe of his shoe. Rock and gravel was loosely piled. When he moved some of it, the rest started sliding.

"Look out!" yelled Matt, but too late. Dirt poured down, right in front of them, shooting up a cloud of dust. The sound of rock and gravel hitting the concrete walls echoed through the tunnel.

The slide stopped as quickly as it had started. Choking on the dust, they climbed over the mound.

"Let me see the flashlight," said Ben. He pointed the beam toward the back wall of the tunnel, where the slide had started. "Oh, man," he said. "Look."

An arm and hand reached out from the fresh mound of dirt and stone, like someone climbing out of a grave. Whoever it was had been there a long time—the hand and arm had rotted down to bones!

Ben stepped closer.

"Don't go near it!" yelled Danny.

Ben wasn't looking at the skeletal hand sticking out of the earth. He was staring at something glinting in the beam of light. Round and shiny, whatever it was lay right next to the arm. He knelt and picked it out of the dust.

"What are you doing?" cried Danny. "Don't touch anything."

"Take it easy," said Ben. "It's a pocket watch." The watch covered the palm of his hand, its gold case permanently sprung open. The arrow hands were missing, lost in time.

"It must have been his," said Matt, pointing at the bony arm.

"Could be a woman," said Danny.

"Nah," said Matt and Ben at the same time.

Ben slipped the watch into his pocket.

"Are you *crazy*?" asked Danny.

"Who's gonna know?" Ben shone the flashlight ahead of them. "C'mon," he said. "Let's get out of here."

Nobody argued.

They walked single file, trying their best to cut through the spi-

der webs with their arms, but the webs crawled all over them anyway, sticking in their hair and all over their arms and backs. Ben thought it was just about the grossest thing that he ever—

Something moved behind them.

"What was that?" asked Danny.

A wailing, like a cry on the wind, seemed to follow them.

"Listen," said Matt.

The wailing grew louder…closer. It was right behind them.

"Come on!" yelled Ben. He still had the flashlight. He started running. Matt and Danny were beside him.

He didn't know how far it was before they'd find the way out. They couldn't go back, not to whatever it was wailing behind them. It wasn't a ghost, thought Ben. Couldn't be a ghost. No way.

The walls started shaking. A loud rumbling rolled through the tunnel, as if the whole thing were about to cave in.

"Hurry," yelled Ben, running right through the spider webs without even brushing them aside. He could feel spiders crawling on him, one right on his face, but he didn't stop to brush it off. Didn't have time.

Ahead, he saw something shimmering like a pale moon. Only when he got closer did he realize that it was an opening, a way out of the tunnel. The walls were still shaking. He could imagine the walls crumbling around him, the earth pouring in, and himself trapped by a landslide just as that man had been!

He ran until he reached outside, breathless and terrified. Only then did he beat at the spiders crawling all over him. Matt and Danny were covered head to foot in the clinging webs too. They looked like ghosts themselves, wrapped in shredded grave clothes.

Ben heard another loud rumbling, and looked to the top of the hillside above them. An eighteen-wheeler thundered down the freeway, making the ground shudder. That's what they'd heard in the tunnel.

He felt dumb to have been so scared. *But what about the wailing?*

Once Matt and Danny left, Ben went home. It had been strange when he first came in the house. Sassy, his small brown and white shelty, had barked and actually *growled* at him. She'd never done that before. He put the pocket watch in his desk drawer with his schoolbooks. When he came downstairs for dinner, Sassy acted normal and wanted to be petted as usual.

All through dinner Ben couldn't get his mind off Death and Dagger. *Whose pocket watch had they found? More importantly, whose body?* He wondered whether he should tell his parents. Was he breaking some law if he didn't report it? He knew his folks would ground him forever if they found out he'd gone into the tunnel. But maybe finding the body was more important…

"You're awfully quiet tonight," said his dad. Ben quickly snapped out of his imagination. His dad worked at Jet Propulsion Laboratory, right next to the flood channel. He'd know if there were any stories about the tunnel.

"Some kids told me about this Death and Dagger place today," said Ben carefully. "Have you ever heard anything about it?"

Surprisingly, his dad laughed.

His mom didn't. "I don't see what's funny, Richard."

His dad stopped laughing with some effort. Three-year-old Sydney wanted to know what was so funny.

"I can't believe kids are still going to that old place," his dad said. "You'd better not be going there if you know what's good for you. It's dangerous."

"I only heard about it from some kids I met," Ben said, trying to sound innocent.

"Death and Dagger used to be a storm drainage tunnel back in the forties," his dad said. "There was an earthquake, and a workman was trapped in there by a cave-in and never found. When I was in high school, kids used to dare each other to go down there, but the city finally sealed it up. It was an interesting place…"

"You went there yourself?" Ben asked, amazed.

"Richard!" said his mom. "Is that the way to keep him safe?"

"Just because I did it doesn't mean you should," his dad back-tracked hastily. "It was foolish of me and my friends. I trust you'll be smarter than to risk your life that way. The whole place is a death-trap waiting to be sprung. Your mother and I would be very unhappy if we found out you'd gone there."

"I was just curious," Ben said, and went back to eating his steak.

Ben spent a lot of time looking at the pocket watch that night. Even though it was old, the gold cast still had a dull shine. He put it in his drawer again reluctantly, still worrying whether or not to tell his parents. If they knew, they'd never let him go out again. When he fell asleep, his dreams were uneasy.

Ben woke to hear his sister yelling at the top of her lungs. By the time Ben got to Sydney's room, his mom and dad were already there. His mom held a frightened Sydney in her arms. His dad held the pocket watch wonderingly in his hand.

"What happened?" Ben asked.

"Do you know anything about this?" asked his dad. The watch case glowed faintly in the dim light. "Sydney had it in her hands when we got here."

"I found it in some bushes today down by Oak Grove Park," Ben lied. "I don't know how Sydney got it. The watch was in my desk drawer."

His dad handed Ben the watch, but eyed him suspiciously.

"Sydney said she saw something big and white in her room," his mom said. She patted Sydney's head reassuringly. "You don't know anything about that, do you?"

Ben swallowed a gasp of horror. *Something big and white...* Sydney was only three. She wouldn't know how to describe a ghost.

The next day, Sunday, was gloomy and cold. Ben felt sick. How had Sydney found that watch? She couldn't have reached his drawer. We never should have taken it, Ben thought. A sick chill spread through his body. *First Sassy growls at me, now Sydney sees a ghost. What's next?* He decided to call Matt and Danny.

"Did you guys notice anything...uh...weird in the last day or so?" Ben asked Matt.

Matt laughed. "Other than Danny actually paying for the comic books he owes me? No," said Matt. "Hey, Danny, anything strange to tell Ben?"

"Nope," said Danny.

Ben jumped as the front door of his house slammed loudly. Before he knew it, the pocket watch was being thrust in his face. His mom grabbed the phone from him. She was clearly angry, and wet from the drizzle outside.

"Hello. Matt? Ben will have to call you back," she said, hanging up the phone.

She turned her attention to Ben. "Your watch nearly caused a terrible accident. I was driving, and someone cut me off at an intersection. I hit the brakes, but they wouldn't go down. Do you know why? Because this was jammed under them!"

"I—I don't know how that got in th-there, Mom," Ben stammered. "It—it was in my desk! Really."

"I don't care what you have to say, young man. I'm furious with you! You're grounded for a week. And no TV. Go to your room. I don't want to see you till dinner!" Mom stormed off, shaking water from her long black hair.

There were no two ways about it, Ben realized. The watch was haunted, and if he kept it, someone in his family was going to get hurt. He had to return it to Death and Dagger, grounded or not. Tonight.

That evening, when Ben snuck out and got on his bike, rain had been coming down in torrents for hours. The noise of the storm covered the sounds of his leaving the house. Also, it didn't hurt that everyone was asleep. It was past midnight, the latest Ben had ever been out on his own. He could feel the weight of the watch within his jacket's inner pocket, pressing against his heart.

Ben rode through the dark trails to the flood channel. Mud splashed up from the bike's wheels, but enough rain sluiced over his slicker to keep washing it off. He wished Matt and Danny were with him, but they hadn't wanted to go out in the storm to crawl in some tunnel. He was alone. As the sign for Death and Dagger came within sight, he felt his loneliness worse than ever.

Ben left his bike propped against the warning sign and turned on the flashlight he'd stowed in his slicker pocket. There it was. The entrance to the tunnel gaped like an open mouth, jagged pieces of concrete ringing the sides with sharp teeth.

Don't want to go down there, Ben thought. He remembered the wailing sound. The skeletal hand. *I've got to,* he told himself. He couldn't put his family in danger anymore because of what he'd done. He didn't let himself think about it any longer. Taking a big breath for courage, Ben jumped into the hole.

He landed, his feet sliding under him in the mud that seeped through the opening. He fell back, hitting his tailbone hard against the floor. *I could have broken an arm or a leg,* he thought, scrambling to his feet. *Then where would I be? Trapped in here, that's where.* The thought stayed with him as he looked into the pitch blackness ahead.

Ben moved forward. His flashlight's tiny beam stabbed into the darkness and at the spider webs with their scuttling occupants, unused to the light. He thought about the workman who'd been buried alive down here, holding his pocket watch as he died.

Watching his time run out.

The darkness before Ben deepened, and he realized he had reached the caved-in section. With as much bravery as he could muster, he crawled over the dirt and concrete.

The skeletal arm and hand still reached out from the earth just as it had before, but strangely, alone in the tunnel, Ben saw everything differently. The skeleton wasn't reaching out to grab anyone. It was reaching out for help.

With care, Ben removed the pocket watch from his slicker. Thoughtfully, he began to wind it. He wound it until the ring at the top wouldn't turn anymore, and in the silence of Death and Dagger, he heard ghostly ticking. With respect, he placed the watch back in the skeletal hand.

"Time's started for you again," Ben said, hoping the spirit of the workman could hear. "You're free to go."

At that instant the tunnel began to shake savagely, and Ben was thrown hard up against the wall. His flashlight smashed into pieces on the floor. The earth rumbled as though it were tearing itself apart. In the complete darkness, all Ben could hear was the roar of concrete beginning to buckle and cave in. *An earthquake,* he realized. *I'm going to be trapped here, just like...*

Ben staggered to his feet, but in the total blackness he couldn't tell which was the right way to go. A chunk of concrete landed next to him. As Ben began to panic, a white shape appeared before him. Instinctively, he ran toward it, slipping and slamming into the wall again and again as the tunnel shook like a rattle in a baby's fist.

The roaring of the earthquake echoed through the tunnel like an enraged bear about to crush Ben with its weight. He felt the breath of fear on the back of his neck as he ran.

Then, there it was—the exit! Leaping for the escape hole with all of his might, Ben grabbed for the crumbling edges of the broken tunnel and pulled himself up and out. Lightning cracked the sky wide open as he knelt exhausted on the still-rumbling ground. Cold rain washed down in a flood from the heavens.

Looking back into the hole, Ben saw the source of the bright light that had led him to safety. A ghostly image of the workman stood in the crumbling tunnel, a sad but relieved smile on his face.

As Ben watched, the ghost took the watch from his shirt pocket and looked at it. The concrete and earth collapsing all around didn't seem to affect him at all. The ghost of the workman stared calmly at Ben.

"Time to go home," he said, and vanished.

Call me a control freak if you like; collaboration has never appealed much to me. The notion of collaborating with my children did sound like fun, however, and so it mostly proved to be—for them as well, I hope.

Matt comments: "Since the idea of writing with my father sank in, I've played an active role in writing this story. At first I was undecided about the setup. These feelings brought new dimensions into the story."

And Tammy says: "Our story began life when Matt and I collaborated on the first couple of pages to get things going, then handed them over to our dad. He altered them and wrote a version of the rest of the piece. After going back and forth and being torn to pieces, the story was finally completed. In writing it, we drew largely on the real life interaction of my brother and me. Realizing your companion is not your sibling (as they are too nice!) is a situation we could envisage—as social pleasantries tend to be rare between me and Matt!"

Indeed, and at first I wondered if I might have to be a referee rather than a collaborator, but we got on together perfectly well. Much that is best in this story belongs to Tammy and Matt, and it was a pleasure to work with them.

THE MAZE

by Ramsey Campbell, Tammy Campbell, and Matt Campbell

✻

Naomi awoke in a four-poster bed and felt as though she were still asleep. She was watching the dawn paint its canopy pink when the door slowly opened.

"Are you awake, Name?" her little brother, Nick, asked.

"No, and don't call me that."

"Yes, you are, Name. This is really some hotel, isn't it? Want to explore?"

"Get off my bed or I'll kick you off. Go and bother Mom and Dad."

"They said to stay away till breakfast. What'll we do?"

Naomi remembered what she'd seen last night from the balcony before going to bed. She kicked off the quilt and padded across a carpet that felt as soft and thick as sand on a beach. She pushed back the heavy curtains. Outside the window, under half a moon, a lawn stretched away into a mist that blurred the English farmland in the distance. At the near edge of the mist, a hedge maze sprouted from the grass.

She saw the pale scalps of two statues beside a stone bench at the center of the maze, and she thought she could trace the way to them just by looking. Then Nick started jumping up and down in his annoying way, distracting her. "I'm going to get dressed," he said, "and then I'll beat you to the middle."

"You'll try. You'll get lost and have to cry for Mom and Dad."

Their parents might be asleep for a while yet; they hadn't slept much on the flight from New York. After Nick had stomped away, she pulled on a track suit and went into the paneled corridor to find him. Outside his room her attention was caught by an oil painting on the wall.

The painting showed a boy and a girl holding hands and wearing old-fashioned clothes. The boy was about Nick's age—eight—and the girl looked two years older, like Naomi herself. Their blond hair was almost white. Their eyes, as green as the hedge maze behind them, seemed to follow her as she tried to move out of their reach. She couldn't help touching the canvas to prove to herself they were only images in a picture—but then she snatched her hand back with a gasp. It must have been the central heating that made the painted girl feel warm as flesh.

Nick came to his door and giggled. "What are you scared of?" he asked Naomi. He poked the chest of the boy in the picture then darted off down the hall.

Naomi wondered whether his quick retreat was due only to his eagerness to be in the maze. Before she raced to the wide staircase, she noticed a plaque below the painting. The children had died at the ages she and Nick were now. The idea made her shiver, and she ran after her brother, out the back door of the hotel.

The early morning smelled of wet grass. The dampness seeped

through her sneakers and chilled her feet as she trod on the lawn. Nick was almost at the entrance to the maze. The moon above reminded Naomi of a half-closed eye that was pretending not to watch their every move. When she joined her brother, he pulled his wraparound sunglasses out of his track suit and stuck them over his eyes.

"You don't look cool—you look stupid," she told him. "I'm not staying with you if you wear those."

"I don't want you with me. Whoever gets to the middle first wins," he gabbled, and darted into the mouth of the maze. She saw him dodge left, and then he was gone.

Naomi smiled to herself. She was almost certain that you had to turn right first to reach the center. She'd seen the proper way from her window. Her brother was likely heading for a dead end. Naomi stepped hurriedly through the maze's entrance—an archway cut into a fat hedge that stood a head taller than her parents. She turned right before Nick could come back and catch sight of her.

The space between the hedges was as wide as her arms could reach. When the mist had retreated into the maze, it had left behind millions of dewdrops. They glittered on the leaves and beaded the grass underfoot. At the end of the first hedge she had to double back on herself, then turn right again almost at once. Now she felt she was really in the maze, where there was nothing but greenery, and it was so quiet she couldn't even hear Nick. "You're going the wrong way, you know," she called, trying to discover where he was.

"You mean you are."

His voice came from somewhere to her left. It must have been all the hedges between the two of them that made him sound so far away. Or was he making himself sound distant to trick her? Had that been Nick she'd glimpsed through a leafless patch of the hedge to her left, a small figure running silently along the lane next to hers? Maybe she and Nick weren't the only children staying at the hotel and exploring the maze.

"I'm not coming to find you if you get lost," she called louder.

"Bet you can't even find yourself."

It hadn't been Nick on the other side of the hedge; he was definitely too far away. She almost told him that they might not be alone in the maze, but he sounded unbearably smug, as if he knew she was following a route that led nowhere. She decided to let him find out for himself.

It did look as though a hedge blocked the way ahead. But when she marched to it, she found it was a T-junction. She swung right at once, and then she stopped, her feet skidding on the grass. A face as pale as the moon—a girl's face, with green eyes—was watching her through a gap in the hedge at the next turn.

Naomi felt she couldn't move until the other girl did. Then the back of her hand brushed the hedge. The wet leaves spilled cold drops down her wrist, and she took a step toward the utterly still figure. She saw at once that it was a statue, almost overgrown by the hedge. The stone girl looked as though she were hiding, lying in wait.

The statue's eyes were covered with bright green moss, but the rest of her face, as far as Naomi could see through the hedge, was bare. She stuck out her tongue at the statue for scaring her, then

she stalked past it. "Don't look back," she muttered to herself.

Naomi was halfway to the maze's next junction when she heard the hedge rustling behind her. She glanced over her shoulder, but she could no longer see the statue, only the leaves shivering where its face had been.

The face had been very like that of the girl in the painting, thought Naomi, particularly the way its eyes seemed to follow her. She wanted to call out to Nick, just to reassure herself that he was there, but she wasn't going to let her little brother think that she was scared. Instead, she ran ahead to the next junction—and found that it led to a dead end. She had to go back. She had to pass that place where the statue was waiting.

Or had it been a statue? She'd seen its face for only a moment, its green eyes watching her. She clenched her fists and forced herself to hurry along the path. She was almost at the bend that hid the pale-faced figure—in another moment, she was past it. There was no sign of the figure at all.

She dashed to the T-junction where she'd turned the wrong way. She was about to flee back to the maze's entrance when she heard Nick shout, "You can't scare me, Name! I know that's you behind there."

He was much nearer the center. He might be a pain, but she couldn't just leave him. "There's someone besides us in here, Nick," she called at the top of her voice. "Don't let them bother you. Go to the middle and I'll meet you there."

"You'll try, you mean."

Was he as unconcerned as he sounded or only pretending?

Naomi didn't know which she'd rather be true. She hurried left, in the direction of his voice, then had to turn right, then left, then right again. She felt as though the maze were taunting her, pretending to lead her to her brother only to force her away from him. But the next bend took her onto a long path. This had to be heading straight for the center, she thought, even if she couldn't see the end of it for the mist.

"I'm coming, Nick!" she called, and began to run.

She expected the mist to fall back as she moved forward, but it stayed where it was. She felt its chill reaching for her. Twigs were creaking and snapping somewhere behind her; but when she turned, all she could see was the mist creeping up. The hedges seemed to be closing in, leaning toward her.

As she ran, she hugged herself to stop the cold wet leaves from licking her hands. She slipped on the grass, and her elbow poked into a prickly hedge. The leaves sprayed her face with icy water. She sucked in a breath to shout to Nick again, but stopped herself.

The mist ahead seemed to be withdrawing, and she saw another junction appear. She sprinted toward it, but the path simply doubled back. There was nowhere else to go.

As she skidded around the bend, she thought a face peered through the hedge at her—a face as white as a skull, with green eyes. She ran, and suddenly there was no path. She had been certain that she was heading away from the center, but now she was there.

She stood on a patch of lawn about twenty feet square, with nothing on it except a stone bench carved with some words and numbers. At first she didn't know why the sight of the place made her shiver, but then she remembered. She'd seen two statues from her window.

She realized now that they hadn't been statues. They'd been white-haired figures standing absolutely still, and now they were stalking through the maze. She saw movement on the path opposite her, and she screamed as the figure stepped out of the mist.

"It's me, Name," he said.

The appearance of Nick was such a relief that she almost didn't say, "Don't call me that or I'll call you Blue Eyes."

Blue Eyes was their parents' nickname for him. For once, though, he didn't seem annoyed at her for using it. "What shall I call you, then?" he asked politely.

"Try Naomi," she snapped. "How did you get over there?"

"I can show you the way," he said, and held out a hand to her.

The gesture seemed odd to Naomi. They hadn't held hands for years. "I told you before," she said, ignoring his outstretched hand, "I'm not walking with you unless you take those stupid glasses off."

"I will, when I've taken you," he said.

"And you can stop talking in that stupid way as well. What do you think you sound like?" She'd had enough of his trying to sound old-fashioned; he must be pretending to be a character in some old film he'd seen. For some reason it did more than irritate Naomi. It made her nervous.

"I'm going back the way I know," she declared and turned to go.

"If you prefer, Naomi."

Naomi now realized that she would have to go back past the

junction where that green-eyed face had been. She was glad that Nick was following her. She slowed her steps, letting him almost catch up before she ventured onto the path.

The tops of the hedges were beginning to glitter as the sun climbed above the invisible hills. Naomi had to squeeze her eyelids to a thin slit to see that there was no face behind the leaves at the corner. After she turned, the straight path appeared. It was clear of mist now, but too narrow for her and Nick to walk side by side. She could hear him just behind her. Then she heard something else: a boy's voice calling, somewhere deep in the maze.

"Name," the voice pleaded. "Naomi."

She shivered and spun around. "Did you hear that, Nick?"

"It's nobody, Naomi."

Nick was giving her a wide smile, but she would have been more reassured if she had been able to see his eyes instead of two miniature portraits of herself in those wraparound sunglasses. "You did hear it, though," she said over her shoulder as she walked faster along the path.

"It's only a voice. It can't do any harm now."

"Did you see him?"

"Who, Naomi?"

"The boy." She wished she hadn't started talking about this until they were out of the maze. But for once she wanted to know what Nick thought about something. "I think I saw the girl."

"Which girl?"

It frightened her to say it, but she had to. "The one from the painting."

"Clarissa. And Henry was her brother."

He'd read their names under the painting, of course. "So what?" Naomi demanded.

"What else do you know about them?"

Naomi didn't like this. Suppose talking about the dead children brought them closer? But before she could change the subject, the voice in the maze called to her again. "Name, where are you? It's me. It's Nick."

"No, you aren't!" she cried out. "You only know our names because you heard us using them. You don't even sound like my brother!"

At least the voice sounded farther away, thought Naomi. But she knew it wouldn't be far enough until she and her brother were out of the maze.

"That's right, Naomi," said Nick from behind her. "We know who he really is, don't we? He may just as well give up."

She didn't tell Nick to talk about something else, because she knew he'd likely refuse to talk about anything at all. As long as Nick kept talking, she wouldn't have to look back to reassure herself that he was behind her. Any second now, she thought to herself, she ought to be able to see the bend in the path. But the mist had gathered ahead of them again.

Naomi narrowed her eyes. She was almost blinded by the sunlight on the hedges and on the mist.

"Shall I tell you what happened?" asked Nick.

At last, the mist drifted backward, and she saw the first bend. "Happened when?" she asked, to keep him talking.

"To Henry and Clarissa."

How could he know? Maybe he'd read it in the brochure, which was left in each of the hotel rooms, or perhaps he was going to make up a story. She followed the path left and waited until he joined her on that stretch. "They died," she said.

"And they were buried here in the maze."

She remembered the carvings on the stone bench—names and dates. She dodged right around the next turn; not many more turns now. "Why would they be buried here?"

"Because they used to play together here. It was their favorite place, until one day when there was a storm. By the time they found their way out of the maze, they were so cold and wet that they caught pneumonia. They knew they were dying, so they made a vow to come back again and be together and live the rest of their lives."

Another left turn, another right, and she was back at the T-junction. The mist was waiting in both directions, and she had to remember which to take. She'd turned left here on the way in. "Right," she muttered to herself, and veered that way, then spoke to Nick. "That doesn't make sense."

"Why not, Naomi?"

Why was he continuing to be so polite? Usually Nick would say anything rather than admit he was wrong. She hurried left, telling herself they were almost out. She felt as though the green of the maze and its chill were closing in around her to slow her down. Then she heard that voice in the depths of the maze. "Don't leave me, Name," it cried. "It *is* me. It's Nick, it's, you know—it's Blue Eyes."

Her brother would never call himself that unless he was desperate, she thought. She swung around as she reached the last bend. The boy she'd been leading out of the maze was just behind her. Before he could move, she snatched off his glasses. His eyes were bright green.

In another moment, the boy's eyes turned blue, but it was too late to fool her. She tried to push past him, but she couldn't bear to touch him, this intruder in her brother's body. She would race around the outside of the maze to find Nick.

She skidded around the bend and saw the hotel. Just as she lunged toward the archway in the hedge that marked the exit from the maze, a girl's white fingers reached through the leaves and closed around her hand.

The fingers were icy as mist. The chill flooded through Naomi, sucked her in, and suddenly she was on the other side of the hedge, watching herself run onto the open lawn and call to the boy who looked like Nick.

"Come back," cried Naomi furiously, but the two children wouldn't listen. They clasped their hands together, skipped across the grass, and vanished into the hotel. Then the hedge around Naomi seemed to thicken before her eyes, and she could see nothing but the maze.

She looked down at herself, at her pale skin and her old-fashioned clothing. Was she trapped forever? If only her parents knew she was here—if she and her brother could make themselves heard before their parents drove away to tonight's destination....

She turned, calling to Nick as she ran back into the maze.

Even though my grandson Brandon is only seven years old, we have already written many stories together. Most of the time we write about things we see. For instance, this summer we spent a week in the mountains in New Mexico. There were wild bears coming near the house, so we wrote about a bear caught in a bear trap.

We got the idea for this story because when Brandon was three he had terrible dreams about wolves. I would help him make signs for his bedroom door warning the wolves to stay away, just as the boys do in our story.

We work on a computer. I type while Brandon gives me ideas. He's very good with dialogue, and he thought of most of what the boys—Scott and Ben—say to each other. He also thought of a way for Scott and Ben to get rid of the wolves.

Even though Brandon knew what the story was about, he found it very scary. We hope you do too. But we also hope you understand that real-life wolves are wonderful, precious animals who should be allowed to live in the wild without fear of being hunted.

Maxine O'Neill   Brandon Apperson

WUFFS

by Maxine O'Callaghan and Brandon Apperson

❖

The first night Benjamin woke his parents, they didn't know what he was screaming about. But his older brother, Scott, knew right away.

Scott sat straight up in bed, his heart pounding.

Lights were going on in the house. Scott heard his mother calling to Ben. "Hold on, honey, we're coming." His father's heavy footsteps hurried down the hallway.

"Wuffs!" Ben cried. "Wuffs!"

The little boy's high-pitched voice shot like an arrow through the darkness.

Ten-year-old Scott had finally started to sleep with the light off. Now he jumped out of bed and quickly turned it on. He got back into bed and pulled the covers up around him. Shivering a little, he listened to his parents calming Benjamin down in the next room. After a few minutes, Ben stopped crying.

Scott's mom came into his room on her way back to bed. "Your brother had a bad dream," she said. "He's okay now, though. Go back to sleep, Scottie."

She kissed him and turned off the light. As soon as she closed the door, Scott turned the light on again. He left it on all night.

❀   ❀   ❀

The next evening Ben was fine, and he didn't talk about his bad dream.

Scott relaxed. He began to think he'd misunderstood his brother's words after all. But the following night, Ben's screaming began again.

"Wuffs! There's wuffs!"

It took much longer for Scott's parents to quiet Ben this time. He was still sobbing when Scott's father opened his bedroom door.

"Are you still awake?" his dad asked.

"Yes," Scott said. "Is Ben okay?"

"He's pretty upset." Scott's dad had a grim look on his face. He came in and sat down on the edge of the bed. "Scott, I want you to tell me the truth. Have you been teasing Ben? Telling him scary stories? Or maybe the two of you were watching a TV movie you weren't supposed to watch?"

"No, Dad," Scott said, his feelings a little hurt.

"You're sure?"

"Yes, I told you. We didn't do anything like that."

"All right. I believe you. It's just so strange. Do you know what he's dreaming about? Wolves, just as you did when you were his age. Did you tell him about the bad dreams you used to have?"

Scott shook his head. "I forgot all about it, Dad."

And he had, most of the time. It had been a long time since he was Ben's age, but it was hard to completely forget the terror he'd once felt.

"Okay, pal," his dad said. "I'm sorry. I never meant to jump on you."

"That's okay," Scott replied.

But Scott was still upset when his doorknob turned a few minutes later and Ben crept into his room, carrying his old blanket. Benjamin was only three years old. He had big blue eyes and blond hair that stuck up all over his head.

"What do *you* want?" Scott asked.

"Mommy and Daddy went to bed," Ben said.

"Yeah? So?"

"I wanna sleep with you," Ben said.

"Well, I don't want you in my bed," Scott said. "You snore like a pig and kick like a horse. I won't get any sleep at all."

"Please," Ben said. "I'm really scared. It's not a dream, Scottie. I saw them outside. They got red eyes and sharp teeth and—"

"Oh, all right, stop whining. You can put your pillow on the bottom of the bed and sleep there. But you'd better not kick me or you're toast. Understand?"

Benjamin nodded. He covered himself with his blanket and curled up at Scott's feet. Soon he was snoring and grinding his teeth. But it didn't matter, because Scott couldn't sleep anyway. He thought back to the time he was three years old. He used to see pairs of red eyes in his bedroom at night too.

Scott shivered. "It was just bad dreams, that's all it was."

The next evening Ben was afraid to go to bed.

"I wanna watch TV," he kept saying. "I wanna play with my toys."

"No, sweetie," his mom said. "It's bedtime. Let's read a story, then I'll tuck you in."

Two minutes later Ben came running out of his room clutching his blanket. His face was pale, and his eyes were huge and fearful.

"The wuffs are coming to get me, Mommy!" he screamed. "Make them go away!"

"Oh, Ben," Mom said. She reached down and picked him up. "I know what we can do. When Scottie was having bad dreams, he put a warning sign on his door. It told the bad wolves to stay away. Remember, Scottie?"

When Scott didn't answer right away, his mom said quickly, "You can help Ben, can't you, Scott? Go help him make a sign for his door."

"Oh, all right," Scott said.

Ben ran and got paper and a pencil, then handed them to Scott.

"Oh, no," Scott said. "You want a sign? You write it yourself."

Ben was only three, but he could print his letters. "Well…okay," he said. "But you gotta help me spell the words. What should I write?"

"It's your dumb sign. You tell me."

Ben thought for a minute. Then, with Scott's help, Ben wrote the words in big letters.

Wuffs Keep Out!
Go Away and Don't Come Back!
This
Means
You!

Scott taped the sign to Ben's door.

"Happy now?" he asked.

Ben nodded.

Scott was just falling asleep when he felt Ben climb up on his bed.

"You could at least ask," he said crossly.

"Can I stay here—please?"

"Okay, but kick me once and you're out. Got it?"

Scott was so tired he fell asleep instantly. But he was woken a little while later by the sound of soft footsteps. Someone was walking around his room. At first he thought it might be Ben, but it was more like the sound an animal might make, a dog or maybe—

A wolf, he thought. He lay very still and listened.

Ben suddenly appeared from under the covers. He was shaking, and his hands and feet were icy cold.

"What's that noise?" asked Ben, pulling on Scott's arm.

"I don't know," Scott replied. "Be quiet."

It was dark in the room. Scott had left the light on when he went to bed, but now it was off. Maybe Mom or Dad had come in and turned it off; he couldn't remember. Now he could hear the sound of panting. Loud, fast panting.

Scott wanted to believe that Ben had been dreaming about the wolves. He also wanted to believe he'd dreamed the wolves up when he was three years old. But now there was no mistaking it. Scott sat up in bed. He could actually see the glowing red eyes in the corner of his room. Moonlight shone in the window and gleamed on sharp white teeth.

"Scottie," Ben wailed softly. He dug his fingers into his brother's arm so hard that it hurt.

"Close your eyes," Scott ordered.

"But they're gonna get us, Scottie."

"I mean it, Ben. Close your eyes right now."

Ben closed his eyes, and Scott did too. "When we open our eyes we won't see anything except furniture and toys and stuff."

"Promise?" Ben asked.

"I promise," Scott answered. "Now say it, Ben. There're no wolves in this room."

"No wuffs," Ben said.

The two boys listened as the sound of panting started to fade away. When the boys opened their eyes, the wolves were gone.

"See?" said Scott. "What did I tell you?"

"They'll be back," Ben said.

At school the next day, Scott was sure he'd flunked his math test. At recess, he just stood around and watched the other kids shooting baskets and having fun.

"What's the matter with you?" his friend Alex asked. "Are you sick or something?"

"Guess so," Scott said.

But Scott wasn't really sick. He was just tired.

For the rest of the day in school, Scott couldn't stop thinking about what had happened in his room the night before.

After school, instead of going to the park to play baseball with his friends, Scott went to the library. First he found a videotape about wolves and watched it on the library television.

"Wolves live in small family groups called packs," the narrator said as the screen showed pictures of the gray furry animals. "Although these shy, beautiful creatures are fierce hunters, they hunt only for food, and stay far away from humans. Once they roamed the mountains and forests of the United States, but now only a handful are left. They live mostly in Alaska and Canada…"

So normal wolves didn't live anywhere near his home in the Arizona desert.

Scott searched for books about monster wolves. He read about werewolves—people who changed into wolves when the moon was full. Then there was the story about the Big Bad Wolf who blew down the little pig's house and ate him up. And there was the wolf who posed as Little Red Riding Hood's grandmother.

People had been afraid of these kinds of monsters for a long time. Maybe it was their fears that somehow made the creatures come to life.

Scott kept reading. He paid special attention to the ways people got rid of monster wolves. Running away seemed to be the thing a lot of people in stories did. Scott wasn't ready to take Ben and run away from home. And he really didn't think a pot of boiling water would work. Besides, people who lived a long time ago might have a pot that big, but his family didn't.

To get rid of a werewolf, you had to kill it with a silver bullet. But his mother wouldn't allow a gun in the house. She didn't even want them to have play guns. The only thing Scott had in his closet was an old popgun. He had used it a few years ago when he dressed up like Davy Crockett for Halloween.

When he was finished reading, Scott closed the last book and pedaled home slowly. Ben was sitting on the floor in the living room staring at a cartoon show on TV, holding his blanket. His hair stuck up in all directions.

"Scott," his mom said. "Can't you play a game or something with your brother? All he wants to do is watch television."

Scott's mother worried a lot about Ben. She would say, "Scottie, you have to take care of your brother." Even though it bugged Scott sometimes, he still watched out for little Ben. He knew Ben was different. He wasn't as tough as Scott had been, even at that age. For instance, any Disney movie could make Ben cry. And the kid even hated to step on ants, for cripes sake.

When Scott was three years old, he got rid of the wolves by telling himself the wolves weren't real. He did this over and over until he believed it. Then the wolves went away. Scott was sure his brother couldn't do this. It was up to Scott to figure out some way to help him.

"Come on," Scott said. He grabbed Ben's hand and dragged him into the bedroom.

"I don't wanna play a game," Ben said.

"We're not playing a game."

"What are we doing then?" Ben asked.

"We're going to figure out a way to get rid of the wuffs."

Scott didn't think his parents would ever go to bed. But as soon as he heard their bedroom door close, Ben came running into Scott's room. His eyes sparkled with excitement.

"Hurry," Ben said. "Get the gun."

"Shhh," Scott warned. "We don't want Mom and Dad back here." He knelt beside the bed, reached under it, and took out the weapon. It was only his popgun, and the "bullets" were made from aluminum foil. But after they had talked about what Scott had learned in the library, they decided this was the way to kill the monster wolves. If silver bullets worked on werewolves, maybe they would kill the wuffs, too.

To make this work, Scott knew they both had to *believe* everything was real.

Scott loaded the weapon. He put it beside him on the bed. Then he took a deep breath, reached over, and switched off the lamp. The room was plunged into a darkness so black it was as if they were swimming in ink.

Ben was huddled beside him. After a minute, he asked, "Do you think they'll come?"

Scott could hear the fear creep into his little brother's voice. A sudden chill trickled down his own back like icy water.

"They'll come," he said.

For a long time, nothing happened. Scott discovered that even terror dies down after a while. Ben fell asleep and even started to snore, and Scott's eyelids were getting heavy when he heard the soft padding of animal feet.

Scott shook his brother awake.

Ben's fingers dug into Scott's arm. "Sc-Sc-Scottie—"

"I see them," Scott said.

Four ghostly images glided through the wooden door and into the room. Their red eyes blinked in the darkness. The sound of their panting made Scott's heart pound wildly. He could almost feel their hot breath on his face. When he picked up the gun, his fingers felt heavy and clumsy.

"We have to do this just like we practiced," he told Ben, and gave his brother a handful of foil bullets.

Scott raised the weapon and looked down the barrel into the terrible red eyes. *If the wolves are real,* he told himself, *then the gun and the bullets are real, too.*

That's when they struck. All four showed their sharp, white teeth and growled angrily as they began to lunge right toward *Ben.*

No! thought Scott as he took aim and fired—once, twice, three times. He reloaded the gun as fast as Ben could hand him the bullets.

He fired again! And he did his best to believe. Believe that this was a real gun. That these were real silver bullets...

And then, slowly, one by one, the four sets of red eyes winked out.

The boys sat very still. For long minutes they heard and saw nothing unusual in the room. All of a sudden, the darkness seemed like nothing more than ordinary night.

"Are they really gone?" Ben whispered.

"Gone for good," Scott said. He turned on the light. "Okay, Ben, you can go on back to your own bed."

Ben just sat looking at him.

"Did you hear what I said? Get moving."

"Couldn't I stay here for tonight? Just to make sure?"

"Oh, all right. But if you kick me in your sleep again—"

"I know," Ben said. "I'm toast."

This was a deeply enjoyable project. Ben has always been a good writer, a fact first demonstrated to me in concrete fashion by "The Big Bet," a story about a Monopoly game he wrote in the third grade. Its first sentence was, "The bet was on." When I read that, I said to myself, "Good, he's always going to be able to take care of himself." I meant it, too. The important things can't be faked, and I thought I was hot stuff when I was in third grade, but I didn't know how to begin a story with a jolt like that. So maybe even if I hadn't been struggling to finish a novel when the time came to write this story, I might have asked him to start it for me, but I suspect that I would not have been that smart.

Anyhow, I was struggling with the end of the novel, and at my request Ben, a senior at Fieldston School in New York, stepped in to get us launched with his characteristic and authoritative snap. When he could spare the time, his beleaguered old man supplied some development. We went on in this way for some months, me staggering away from the novel whenever Ben supplied me with more pages. He gave this story its best, most shining detail, but I am not about to tell you what it is. He wrote the ending a few days after I finally limped across the finish line of my novel, after which I added my thoughts, and then we were done. Both of us like this story, and both of us think that "D" and his creepy friends deserve what they get.

IN TRANSIT

by Peter Straub and Benjamin Straub

※

Around one-thirty on a rainy Sunday afternoon in November, the Pruitts found themselves on the road once again. Jack Pruitt, an ex-cop, ex-bartender, ex-carpenter, ex- a lot of things, rocketed his gray car down the interstate. His eleven-year-old son leaned brooding against the passenger door. Sammy had moved as far from his father as he could get and still stay on the front seat.

Sammy hated to move. Just when it seemed possible for him to make new friends, the Pruitts had to leave all over again. Ten miles out of Southport and their last—their fiftieth? their sixtieth?—apartment, Sammy had told his father how much he hated starting a new school only to move on a few months later.

Jack Pruitt could console his son only by saying, as he had too many times before, "Moving is something we have to do, kid. You might not enjoy it, but I know you understand it. Anyhow, it can be nice to meet new people."

It's never nice to meet new people, Sammy thought, staring at the dark nothing outside the window. *I wish we could be like the others.*

Sammy's father drove on through the night, turning his eyes from the road only to look at his son. The miles rolled on, seventy miles out of Southport, then eighty, and the night continued. The next thing Sammy knew, he was waking up to his father's voice.

"Sammy! Wake up, old boy. We're here."

Sammy wiped sleep out of his eyes and looked through the windshield. They were in the parking lot of something called the Briar Cliff Motel, a string of cabins attached to an office with a neon sign in the window. It was still night, but the darkness was beginning to turn gray. "What's it called again, Dad?"

"Richland Center. Sounds like an all-right little burg," said Jack Pruitt, grinning as he ruffled his son's hair. "Richland Center, prepare to meet the Pruitts."

Sammy frowned. "I don't like it already. It's going to be just like Southport."

"Maybe it will, maybe it won't. You're going to like it here. Both of us will."

Sammy did not respond. He watched his father get out of the car and pull two of their three suitcases off the backseat. Then in the cold beginnings of dawn, Sammy joined his father. Together they went to the desk and checked in.

For an eleven-year-old boy, Sammy Pruitt had a wide experience of places like the Briar Cliff. Usually, he and his father had to sleep on the same sagging mattress in the same rotten double bed. All they ever got on the television, if they were lucky enough to have a television, were three local channels so wiggly with distortion that they had to grab the antenna to see anything at all.

But this room was better than almost any of the others. First, it was big enough to walk around in without running into a wall as soon as you got started; and second, it had two, count 'em, *two,* double beds. But the best reason was that it had a working television set with *cable.* Knockout reception on sixty channels!

The day after they checked in, Sammy zigzagged, pole-vaulted, broad-jumped between channels. He leaped from TNT's reruns to *Leave It to Beaver* and *Ren and Stimpy* to infomercials about Psychic Friends. He flipped from a Mel Gibson movie to Stone Temple Pilots on MTV to someone named Julia blinking into the camera on *All My Children,* and then, quickly, accidentally, to CNN, where a lady was talking about what had happened in Southport.

No. Sorry, but no. Not that.

Sammy punched LC for "last channel," where Julia was still blinking back tears, then he stabbed two random buttons, which delivered him into a black-and-white basement. A popeyed fat man and an impatient thin man, whom he recognized—thanks to his father—as Abbott and Costello stood with their backs to a slowly opening crate.

No, no thanks, sorry. You're great, but no, not that, either.

Sammy returned to MTV, where Steven Tyler was flaring his lips over an astonishing amount of teeth. A key slid into the door's lock, and his father came into the room, carrying a huge brown bag. An odor flowed out from the bag in almost visible waves. It made Sammy realize how hungry he was. Food, yes, food—television had made him forget about hunger. Cheeseburgers weren't *real* food, but they would certainly do.

"Hey, kiddo," Jack Pruitt said. "You must be starving. I'm sorry,

I'm later than I thought I'd be, but you'll be glad to know that with hard work, luck, and influence, I lined up almost everything we're going to need. Including lunch. What's that racket?"

"Aerosmith. They're okay, for a bunch of old guys."

"Sure they are," said Jack, trading the bag for the remote control. Sammy wasn't surprised when his dad zeroed in on the Abbott and Costello movie.

"*Abbott and Costello Meet Frankenstein*. Great movie, one of the all-time classics. Food okay?" asked Jack.

"Yeah," Sammy said.

"I have some good news." Jack's gaze remained on the screen. "Richland Center might just turn out to be home, sweet home."

"You found a place already?"

"I did more than that. The big three are all wrapped up." He ticked them off on his fingers. "I found a place. I have a job. I got you into a school. Tomorrow, we move into the bottom half of a really nice duplex, furnished like a real home. It's not far from here, and it's a great price. Every year more and more people leave Richland Center and fewer come in. The people who own the building were afraid they'd never find a renter. The second I walked in, they just about handed me the keys. 'Do you have a job here, Mr. Pruitt?' they asked, and I said, 'Maybe you know Tom Alvin. He's a foreman over at so-and-so, old friend of mine, he'll get me in any time I want.' And he will. Tom will take care of me."

Sammy nodded. As long as he could remember, there had been Tom Alvins, all of them ready to help his father. Sometimes his dad had been a Tom Alvin and placed newcomers in jobs. People like

Dad were like brothers—they all helped each other.

"Here comes the best part," Jack said. "Starting tomorrow, you're a sixth grader at Josiah Walker Middle School, only two blocks away from our apartment. This school is okay. Classes are small because young people have been moving out of town, so they're happy to have a new face. They won't ask too many questions. I talked with the vice-principal and promised that he'd be getting your transcript from Southport in a couple of weeks."

"What happens when they don't get it?"

"You know," Jack said. "The same thing that always happens. People don't want to make trouble. Sooner or later, they'll forget about it. I'd love to settle down for a while, wouldn't you? And wait till you see that house! It makes Southport look like a slum."

"Does it have cable?" Sammy asked.

"Tell you what," Jack said. "If it doesn't, I'll get it for you."

"Southport was on CNN," said Sammy.

"Sure, for thirty seconds. Sooner or later, everybody forgets."

Bela Lugosi and Boris Karloff were stalking Abbott and Costello through a black-and-white castle. Sammy thought that all four actors looked like tired old men, and the castle looked like cardboard. If you leaned against one of those cardboard walls, the whole thing would fall apart.

"I hope the kids will like me," Sammy said. "What's the name of that school again?"

"Josiah Walker Middle School. Sixth grade through eighth grade. After that, they go to Richland Center High." Jack turned to his son and stroked his back. "Maybe this is it. Maybe we'll be able to stay here, and we can see you into high school. It happens. Tom Alvin has been here ten, fifteen years."

Sammy did not want to think about Tom Alvin. He already knew all about him, and Tom Alvin might be gone tomorrow. "Our place is two blocks from the school?"

"That's right."

"Maybe I could invite some kids back? If it's like a real home?"

"I think that would be great." Jack smiled at Sammy. "You're not in love with this movie, are you?"

"This movie sucks," Sammy said. "Sorry."

"Would you like to go outside for a while? Take a stroll with the old man through our new hometown?"

"I'd like to go out by myself," Sammy said.

"Stick close to the motel." Jack stretched out his legs and laughed at the screen. "You know, we deserve cable TV."

"Sometimes I wish we could be like everybody else," Sammy said.

"I did too, when I was your age. Don't go too far away, okay?"

"Whatever, Dad," Sammy mumbled, and ventured out the door.

An exit off the highway joined the road directly in from the motel, and for a moment Sammy thought about seeing if he could run through the traffic and make it to the other side. But he decided not to try. Instead, he walked down the row of vacant cabins and around to the soda machine on the side of the office.

He pushed three quarters into the slot and pressed the lime-green Mountain Dew button. He grabbed the can, popped the top and wandered around to the back of the office. A rusty swing set stood on the sparse lawn, one of its three swings wrapped around the bar at the top. Near the back door, a Ping-Pong table had been set up on a cement patio. The paddles had been tossed carelessly under the table. Someone opened a can of soda behind him, and Sammy spun around.

A heavyset boy who looked a year or two older gave him a nasty grin—*gotcha!*—and tilted the can over his mouth, downing the entire thing in three long swallows. He threw the can to the ground and let out an enormous belch. Sammy would have sworn that one of the swings moved. The boy was one of those people who are born to be outsized and have no choice in the matter. His head looked about a foot wide, and it went straight down into his neck. His waist was as big around as his thick chest, and his pale arms bulged out of the sleeves of his T-shirt.

"Hey, wanna play Ping-Pong? I'll kick your butt." At the same time, the kid sounded overwhelmingly confident and just about as bright as a brass doorknob.

"Sure, but I don't see the…"

"The ball?" A sneaky grin flashed across his face. "Well, that's on accounta cuz I got it right here." He fished in his pocket and pulled out a scuffed Ping-Pong ball.

"All right, let's play," Sammy said, feeling a little nervous about this new acquaintance.

The boy waddled to the table and bent down for the paddles. "What's your name?"

"I'm Sammy, Sammy Pruitt. Me and my dad just moved here." He hesitated a second, and then added, "From Norwalk."

"Oh, great, a new kid, just what we need." His features tightened in irritation, and he fired the paddle across the patio so forcefully that it nearly struck Sammy's face before he could snatch it out of the air. "My friends call me D. My dad owns this dump." He flapped his paddle at the row of depressing cabins. "So I get to live here all year round. It stinks. You gonna go to school here?" He banged the ball to Sammy. Sammy hit it back across the sagging net, and for some time they concentrated on their rally.

When Sammy missed a shot, he retrieved the ball and said, "Yeah, I'm starting at this school tomorrow."

"Walker Middle?"

"No, I think…yeah, that's it. Josiah Walker Middle School."

"What grade are you in?"

"Sixth."

"Me too—Miss Ryan's homeroom. Lucky for you that you met me. You get to walk into school on your first day and brag about knowing the coolest kid in the place. I guess we'll be seeing a lot of each other, little Sammy. I guess we'll be buddies." The same smirking grin twisted his mouth.

Sammy understood that this kid was making fun of him. D didn't think that Sammy was lucky to have met him, and he didn't think they would be buddies. Someone like D only wanted friends who'd do everything he told them to do. What kind of a nickname was D, anyhow? thought Sammy. It probably stood for Dolt.

"Come on, at least try to hit the ball," D said, and for a time they played. D sent a flat, hard drive to the corner of the table and chuckled at Sammy's frantic, useless attempt to return it.

"I'm the most popular kid in school," he said, with the air of explaining an obvious truth to a slow learner. "The way it goes is, all the girls are nuts about me, and all the boys are afraid of me. Just like you. I scare you, don't I, little Sammy?"

Sammy, who was not scared, felt a grim familiar unhappiness. It would've been nice if the kids in Richland Center had been friendly and tolerant to newcomers. Sometimes it happened that way. But more often, in Sammy's wide experience, the students at his new schools froze out a new arrival. In rare cases, when jerks had too much power, they'd even try to make his life miserable.

Here, standing on the other side of the Ping-Pong table, was a prime example of a Class A jerk. Even worse, a Class A jerk who thought he was tough. Sammy hoped that the rest of Miss Ryan's class despised D-for-Dolt, but he was probably too big for that.

"No, you don't scare me," Sammy said. He sighed and looked out over the patchy ground behind the cabins. "Want to prove how strong you are? Show me you can tip over those crummy swings— then I'll really be scared."

Anger flared in D's face. "You think I'm an idiot? My dad would kill me." He moved away from the table, saw that the paddle was still in his hand, and tossed it under the table. "I gotta go in for dinner, but I'll be seeing you tomorrow, sucker. We're going to have fun. Yeah, we'll have a real good time." He gave Sammy his nasty smile and banged through the back door of the office.

Sammy dropped his paddle on the table and went back around the building and down the row of doors to his room, where his father was still lost in Abbott and Costello.

"Anything happen out in the great big world?"

"I met a kid." Sammy dropped into a chair. "We're in the same homeroom."

"Oh?" Jack looked at him and nodded, clearly seeing that things hadn't gone well. "Like that, huh? I'm sorry. How bad was it?"

"I can handle it," Sammy said.

"He's just one kid," said his dad. "Wait until you see the whole class; it'll be a different story."

Sammy shrugged without meeting his dad's eyes.

"So what was this specimen like, anyhow?"

"He called me little Sammy and said I should be afraid of him."

"Didn't understand you very well, did he?" Jack said.

The next morning, Jack drove Sammy to his first day at Walker Middle. Jack would spend the day moving their few things into the bottom half of the rented duplex and putting in some work at Becker Tool & Die, where Tom Alvin was a day shift foreman. Jack told Sammy he'd pick him up at three-fifteen to take him to their new house. After this day, Sammy would walk to and from school.

Sammy's dad went into the school with him, introduced him to the principal and the vice-principal, and came along upstairs to Miss Ryan's room.

To Sammy, Walker Middle was different from most of the other schools he'd passed through in only two things: the small number of students moving toward their classes, and the color of the cinder block walls. The walls were a pale blue instead of the usual swamp green or yellowish white; otherwise, its long corridors lined with lockers, bulletin boards, and Art Department paintings could have been borrowed from any of his last half-dozen schools.

The vice-principal led them to Mrs. Ryan's door and told Jack that everything was going to be "just fine," and that Sammy was going to feel right at home. Jack shook the man's hand, smiled at Sammy, and was gone.

Everything did work out just fine, at least until twelve-thirty. The twenty-one sixth graders in Miss Ryan's homeroom went here and there through the corridors, stopping in one room for math, another for English, yet another for history. This last subject was taught by Miss Ryan herself—a vague, fluttery woman in a purple dress who spent half of Sammy's first class talking about the trouble she was having with her car.

Sammy had already read most of the stories they were to discuss in English. He was ahead of the math class, and Miss Ryan was not going to present any problems. At noon, the sixth and seventh graders went to the cafeteria for lunch—this day's menu was Sloppy Joes and string beans.

Sammy collected his dripping sandwich, his beans, and a half-pint carton of milk, and sat alone at the back of the cafeteria. He saw that the seventh graders pretty much dominated the center of the room. They divided into cliques, whispered and joked with each other, and wandered between their tables to talk and flirt. It was exactly like every school Sammy had ever attended.

Up at the front of the room, the sixth-grade students were much quieter. D and two other boys, Harry and Tod, sat at the far right end of the first table, separated by several empty places from the rest of the class.

Harry was tall and skinny, and his front teeth protruded, like a beaver's. Tod had blond hair and wide-set blue eyes. He would have been nice-looking, except for the perpetual scowl that drew down the corners of his mouth and pulled his eyebrows together.

These three boys, D, Harry, and Tod, always sat together at the back of their classes, apart from the others. Muttering and chuckling to each other, they made no secret of their contempt for both the rest of the class and the teachers, who usually pretended they were not in the room.

During the morning classes, Sammy saw that half of what D had told him was the truth. The boys really were afraid of him. They behaved like sheep penned up with a wolf, veering around him in the corridors, hanging back, fleeing from his approach. But the girls didn't love him, as he'd bragged. They were afraid of him too.

At twelve thirty, a noisy crowd of eighth graders burst into the cafeteria for their lunch period. All the younger students at the tables stood up to return their trays to the counter, get their coats, and file out to the playground.

Most of the seventh-grade boys immediately ran to the basketball court, which took up the back half of the playground. The girls in Sammy's class wandered with the seventh-grade girls toward a corner next to the school and, separating into groups of three or four, sat down on the asphalt or stood in tight circles.

The remaining boys went to the opposite side of the playground and leaned against the tall chain-link fence. D and his friends started toward them. But as they ambled a little less than half the distance, they turned around and looked at Sammy.

Sammy was walking toward a spot at the end of the fence. Two boys, Mike Cooper and Jimmy Thompson, were standing there. They had been friendlier than the others during morning classes.

"Little Sammy!" D called out, and skinny Harry broke into a grin, which showed even more than usual of his long buckteeth. Tod jammed his hands into his coat pockets and glared at him. "Hey, Sammy, don't waste your time on those losers. Come over here. Harry wants to tell you something."

Harry giggled. He looked like a skeleton covered with a very thin layer of flesh.

Sammy stopped moving, aware that everyone but the basketball players was watching them, even the girls. He looked over at Mike Cooper and Jimmy Thompson. The two met Sammy's eyes for a moment and then began drifting up the fence.

"Okay," Sammy said and walked toward them. Tod took his hands out of his pockets and stepped forward. Harry did the same. Sammy came up to the three boys.

D smiled at him. "What was that thing you wanted to tell little Sammy, Harry?"

"Little Sammy, your teeth are funny," Harry said.

"Look who's talking," returned Sammy.

Harry's arms flashed out and pushed him into Tod, who grasped his arms and held him steady.

"Let me go," Sammy said.

"But you shouldna said that to Harry," said D. "Just like you shouldna told me to tip over my dad's swings. We don't like new kids in the first place, and you're a new kid who goes around acting like a big deal."

Okay, Sammy thought, *let's see what happens.* "I don't think I'm any big deal," he said. Tod tightened his grip on his arms.

"You got that part right," D said. "Show him, Harry."

Harry moved up to him and hit him in the stomach. Sammy grunted and bent over. When Harry stepped back, Sammy pulled away from Tod's hold and charged forward. Startled, Harry fell down with Sammy on top of him. Sammy struck him a few times before both D and Tod pulled him off and began to pummel him.

Sammy raised his arms, ducked sideways, and hit the side of D's head with his left fist. D wobbled backward, his face blank with surprise. Sammy ignored the weightless blows that Harry was giving to the side of his chest, and he closed in on D. Then Tod grabbed his ankles and pulled them up. Sammy dropped onto the asphalt, and the three boys circled in and started kicking him. All he could do was draw himself into a ball and wait for it to be over.

Finally, the kicking stopped. His hips and sides ached, and a spot in his lower back sent out steady waves of pain. Slowly, he uncurled and got to his feet. Tod lowered his head and moved a step backward. Leaking tears from his muddy eyes, Harry snarled at him. D was rubbing the side of his face. "Sammy, you don't know how to act, and we're gonna have to teach you. You belong to us. Me and my friends, we're gonna have fun with you."

"Why don't you just try leaving me alone?" Sammy said. "It'll work out better that way."

"Like we listen to you," Harry said.

D went on rubbing his face. "After school, you'll find out how we leave you alone."

For the rest of the afternoon, the three boys trailed behind Sammy between classes, whispering what they were going to do to him after school. That is, D and Harry talked, and Tod grunted. Tod never said anything at all. He was the ultimate henchman.

During the afternoon classes, D and his sidekicks kept up their usual sneering comments from the back of each classroom, but now everything they whispered to each other was about Sammy. He knew what they were doing— besides trying to frighten him. They were warning the rest of the class, especially Mike Cooper and Jimmy Thompson, to stay away from the new boy. It worked, too. By the last class, social studies, Sammy sat alone, surrounded by empty desks.

At the bell, D and his friends slammed their books shut and sped out into the hallway. Some of the others looked at Sammy as they left the classroom, but no one spoke to him. He went to his locker, put on his coat, and shouldered his knapsack.

Students streamed through the halls, happy to be released for the day. Sammy went through the front door with the crowd and fell in behind a small group of eighth graders who were walking toward the sidewalk in front of the school. He heard someone call his name and turned his head to see D, Harry, and Tod lounging against a tree on the school lawn. They began moving toward him.

His father's car pulled up to the sidewalk. "Little Sam-my," Harry sang. "Come here, little Sammy."

Jack got out of the car, saw his son, and smiled. He began walking up the path. "How was the first day?" he asked.

The three boys stopped moving.

"Not so good," Sammy said. He walked up to his father. D's little gang began moving toward the sidewalk.

Jack bent down to look at his face. "Worse than not so good, maybe?"

"Pretty bad."

"Those three lunkheads over there?" Jack nodded toward D and the other two, who were now wandering down the sidewalk, glancing back with little smirks. "They gave you a hard time?"

Sammy nodded. "They ganged up on me in the playground. I was doing all right until I was on top of the tall one, and then they pulled me off and started kicking me."

"Isn't there a teacher out there?"

"No. And all the kids are afraid of them."

"Oh, boy." Jack sighed and hugged him. "Did they hurt you?"

"Only a little." A six-inch patch low on his back still ached, but most of the other pains had faded into dull, throbbing annoyances.

"Well, there are a couple of ways to handle this," Jack said. "Let's talk about it in the car. I can promise you one thing—you're going to love our new place."

Sammy's dad was right. Their new home was on the first floor of a handsome, two-story stone building. It had a bow window, a wide porch, and comfortable, spacious rooms furnished with ornate, old-fashioned chairs, tables, and sofas. Sammy marveled at the size of his bedroom, wondrously equipped with a big television set wired for cable. This was the nicest apartment the Pruitts had found in a long time, nicer than anything since the top half of a similar duplex in Denver, which the six-year-old Sammy had thought as a good as a palace—and maybe nicer than that.

His father wanted to stay in this splendid place for at least a year, if they could manage it, and Sammy did too. Jack liked his work, which paid better than his last few jobs. In most ways, Richland Center was perfect for them. If they handled the school situation in the right way, maybe they could have their year.

"I'll talk to the principal tomorrow," Jack said. "Once we get those three dummies to leave you alone, you'll be able to make some friends, and we can have a nice, peaceful time in this town."

"I sure hope so," Sammy said.

Then there was a knock at the door. When Jack opened it, in came Bill and Sarah Turner, the white-haired couple from upstairs, with a big plate of freshly baked chocolate chip cookies. Richland Center seemed even more perfect than it had before.

After the Turners had gone, Jack took another cookie off the plate and held it up in front of his face instead of immediately biting into it. "You know, we could always try inviting D and his pals over here for dinner. That might turn things around too. It's always worth being as friendly as possible for as long as you can. You said you'd like to have some kids for dinner."

"It might work," Sammy said, without much conviction. Three times in the past, he had invited classmates back to his house. Twice, Jack had even fed them dinner.

"Just remember this, Sammy," Jack said. "It's all up to them."

Smiling, he took a bite out of the cookie.

An eighth-grade girl came to Mrs. Ryan's door during homeroom the next morning and gave her a note. Mrs. Ryan unfolded the note and said that David Meers, Harold Winks, and Tod Grossman were wanted in the principal's office. Groaning, they threw their books together and slouched out of the room.

Fifteen minutes later, the three boys came into math class and turned to Sammy with what seemed a single glare before giving the pass from the principal to the teacher. The teacher glanced at the pass before waving the boys to their seats.

"Sammy's in trouble," D said under his breath.

In a bored voice, the math teacher asked, "What was that, David?"

"Sorry to cause trouble," D said. Harry snickered.

"I believe that's a first," the teacher said, and several of the girls tittered until D stared them down.

As if by accident, the trio jostled Sammy in the corridors between classes, bumped him into the lockers, stepped heavily on his feet. After English class, Harry pushed a folded sheet of paper into his hand. Sammy stepped aside and opened it up. Crude block letters said YOUR DED MEAT. He looked up. Six feet away, D and Harry were watching him with little half-smiles, while Tod was frowning with concentrated rage.

"Harry can't spell," Sammy simply said.

"There's important things you don't learn in school," D said. "Like not being a squealing rat. Your old man can't save your butt this afternoon." He whirled away, and the others followed.

At lunchtime, Sammy again took the table at the back of the room. From their place at the end of the first table, his three enemies regarded him in their separate ways. Harry grinned at him, D smirked, and Tod sent out concentrated waves of malice.

At three-fifteen the final bell went off, and the entire school raced to lockers and then out the front door. Sammy deliberately hung back until almost everyone else had left. D, Harry, and Tod were standing in front of the tree again. When Sammy came outside, they straightened up, preparing to chase him if he decided to run.

Instead of running, Sammy left the path and walked toward them. The three boys stepped forward. D was rubbing his hands together. Harry opened his mouth in a silent laugh.

"Boy, oh boy," D said. "You tried to get *me* into trouble? You had your daddy call Jonesy, the big bad principal? You really thought you could get *away* with that?"

"You thought you could get away with ganging up on me," Sammy said.

"Little Sammy," D said. He shook his massive head. "By next week, you're going to be begging me for permission to breathe."

"Haw haw haw," went Harry.

"Come with us," D said. "There's a cool little vacant lot across the street. We'll do this off school grounds, so big bad Jonesy can't say nothin' about it."

"Big bad Jonesy," Harry said. "El Dorko."

"All right," Sammy said. "Where is this cool vacant lot?"

D raised his hand and pointed past the tree to a side street. "Over there. You're gonna—"

All three boys were looking across the street. Sammy let his pack slip off his shoulder, dipped his knees, and swung his right fist up into Tod's jaw. The kid dropped to the ground like a fallen tree.

Shaking out his throbbing hand, Sammy turned toward D, who was blinking his eyes in disbelief while still pointing toward the vacant lot. For maybe half a second, D recovered enough to register fury, and then Sammy bent forward, stepped in, and drove the same hand deep into his gut. D grunted and staggered backward into Harry, clutching his stomach. He fell to his knees, then collapsed onto his side.

Both Sammy and Harry looked down at D. He lay curled on the ground with his hands over his stomach, his face turning bright red as he struggled for breath. Harry looked back up at Sammy and said, "That's cheating." Sammy came toward him, but Harry spun around and ran off, his skeletal arms and legs flapping in his baggy clothes.

That evening, when Jack asked him how things were going at school, Sammy told him that everything was probably going to be all right from now on.

And for a week it seemed that everything really would be all right. Tod showed up the next day missing two teeth and showing a big purple bruise on his jaw. D glowered at Sammy but otherwise left him alone. Harry lifted his head to examine the ceiling whenever Sammy glanced at him. They avoided him in the halls and at recess sulked alone in a corner of the playground.

After two days, the rest of the sixth grade began to relax and loosen up. They spoke more freely in class and chattered during lunches. During recess, they little by little began leaving the fences to wander through the center of the playground, territory D and his friends had claimed as their own.

On the third day of freedom from tyranny, Mike Cooper and Jimmy Thompson started talking to Sammy, and Sammy told them a carefully constructed version of his life before Richland Center. Then, after the seventh day, the temporary peace ended.

They came out of an alley and caught Sammy from behind as he was walking home. Tod gripped his arms and D struck him in the face before he could pull away. Snarling, Harry hit the side of his head with an empty soda bottle.

The sudden pain paralyzed Sammy while D struck him again. Sammy tore himself away from Tod and sent D reeling back with a blow to his chest, but Harry brought the bottle down on the top of his head, and he went to his knees. Then Tod kicked him solidly in the back and sent him sprawling, and after that all three of them capered around him, landing kick after kick after kick. Before they ran laughing down the street, D leaned over Sammy and said, "Every day, little Sammy. Every day."

That night, Sammy and Jack had a long conversation. At its end, Jack, who really had hoped to spend a long, peaceful time in Richland Center, said, "Nothing lasts forever. You know what to do. I'll make sure everything's ready."

Before the start of homeroom the next day, Sammy came up to

his three attackers in the hall. They gave him amused, superior looks. For about a second, even Tod managed to look amused.

"He's gonna beg for mercy," D said. "Sorry, you're dog meat."

"You're gone," Harry said.

"I'd like you to come to my house for dinner tonight," Sammy said. "All three of you. Maybe we can work things out."

D snorted. "He's trying to buy his way out with food," D said. "What kind of food you got, anyhow?"

"Anything. Fried chicken, steaks, burgers, whatever you like."

Smiling, D considered the offer. "Anything?"

"Anything."

"Cheeseburgers with bacon? Two apiece?"

"If that's what you want."

D nodded. "Hey, I'll eat your food. It don't make no difference—all I ever get at home is franks and beans, so yeah. You guys?"

Tod merely nodded. Harry said, "I want French fries and ice cream, too."

"Okay," Sammy said. "Cheeseburgers with bacon, fries, and ice cream. You like butterscotch?"

"Me and Harry do," said D. "Tod only likes vanilla."

"We'll get both," Sammy said. "Come over around five-thirty." He told them his address.

"It still don't make no difference," D said.

"You might change your mind after you get there," Sammy said, and left them in a state of high hilarity.

A few minutes after five-thirty, the doorbell rang three times, then, almost immediately, twice more. Sammy opened the door, smiling a little more widely than his visitors might have expected.

"I don't know what *you're* so happy about," said D.

"I'm just sorta surprised you guys showed. My dad thought you might be too nervous."

"Yeah, sure, little Sammy, we're nervous," said D. "Just start bringing on the food. We're hungry. You got it right, I hope. Cheeseburgers, that's what we want."

"With bacon," Harry said. "Plus fries. And ice cream."

Sammy smiled again, and said, "I got everything you asked for. And butterscotch and vanilla ice cream. That's cool, isn't it?"

Impatient, D looked past his head, trying to see into the apartment. "You gonna let us in or not, wimp?"

"Give me a second." Sammy grinned again. He stepped back, and the three boys crowded into the entry. Sammy cracked open the inner door and peeked in. "Are you ready, Dad?"

Jack was folding the ladder. "Now I am. Show your friends in."

"Come on in, guys," Sammy said. "Make sure you wipe your feet on the mat. My dad likes to keep a really clean house."

They pushed past him through the inner door and stumbled in together. Then they stopped moving. D surveyed the room. Harry giggled. "Hey, Sammy," D said. "What's with all this paper?"

Newspapers covered the living room and dining room floors, and most of the walls. Bulges showed where the newspapers had been taped over pictures and mirrors.

Harry said, "I don't get it."

Tod wandered toward a wall to touch the newspapers.

"This is creepy," D said. "Place looks like a horror movie."

Smiling, Jack came forward. "You must be the one they call D."

D nodded.

"The truth is, we're only renting this place, and I want to keep it spotless. We don't want grease from the burgers or any ice cream getting on the rugs." He looked at the walls. "And the place just had a fresh paint job. You know, some kids make a terrible mess, even if they try not to." He glanced meaningfully at Sammy, who looked back and smiled.

"Come into the dining room, guys, sit down, make yourselves at home." Jack extended his arm toward the arch at the end of the room. The boys moved slowly past him, and Jack locked the front door. While they glanced uneasily back and forth from him to themselves, he also locked the inner door. "Nothing to worry about," he said. "I always feel safer when the doors are locked."

D hesitated, staring at the locked door, and Jack said, "Come on kids, grub! Big, fat juicy bacon cheeseburgers! Great French fries, *perfect* French fries! Which one is Harry?"

Like a first grader, Harry tentatively raised a hand, then quickly lowered it.

"You're the French fry boy, aren't you? Get in there, you'll love them." He moved in beside the two boys, put his hands on their shoulders, and urged them forward. Tod scowled at Sammy and trudged along behind.

"D, as the big guy around here, you get the place of honor," Jack said. "Head of the table." He pulled out the chair. After a second of hesitation, D sat down. "Sammy and I will sit on either side of you, and your two friends beside us. Tod?" He pointed to the seat next to Sammy. Tod and Harry took their places, and Sammy and Jack got into their chairs. Smiling, Jack turned to Harry, but said nothing for a long time. Harry started to sweat.

"What's wrong with my manners?" Jack finally said. "Here we all are, waiting to eat, and no food. I'll be right back."

Three pairs of eyes followed him into the kitchen. Almost instantly he returned, carrying a platter with six big cheeseburgers, an enormous bucket of French fries, three bottles of ketchup, and soft drinks. The boys looked relieved. Jack put the platter in the middle of the table. "Dig in, guys."

D reached first, and the other two followed. They had devoured most of their first cheeseburgers and half the fries before they noticed they alone were eating. "Where's yours?" D asked.

"Don't worry about us," Jack said. "We want you boys to enjoy yourselves."

D shrugged and went on cramming in food.

Harry had been staring at Jack. "You have the same kind of teeth he does," he said, pointing at Sammy.

"Runs in the family," Jack said. "Have some more fries, my boy."

They ate hurriedly, barely chewing before they swallowed, smearing the French fries through puddles of ketchup and ramming them into mouths already full. It took them no more than twenty minutes to finish their silent meal. Their mouths were smeared with grease, and they were breathing hard. "Love seeing hungry boys eat," Jack said. "Ready for your ice cream?"

D burped. "I don't want no ice cream."

"You're done?" Jack looked at each boy in turn. "Had enough?"

"Yeah," Harry said. Tod nodded.

"Then I guess it's our turn," Jack said. "Sammy?"

Instantly, Sammy was out of his seat and sinking his teeth into Tod's neck. Tod screeched, tried to push him off, and went limp. By that time, Jack had gripped D's arms in his powerful hands and was lifting him off his chair. Holding the wriggling D as if he weighed no more than a kitten, Jack smiled at Harry and said, "I guess you're dessert, Harry."

Harry slipped off his chair in a dead faint.

Jack gave a sigh of deep satisfaction and tasted real food for the first time since they had come to Richland Center.

Late that night, the Pruitts were on the road again, in transit to whatever the next place would be.

Nora: We came up with the idea for this story by thinking *simple* and *scary.* We knew that a typical fear of young kids is monsters in the closet. So we took this idea and gave it a twist. Green, hairy monsters were too corny, so we came up with something that was more evil than any slobbering monster.

While one of us brainstormed ideas, the other would write them down on the computer, leaving gaps and jumping ahead. But we could always go back and fill in the holes.

Matt: Nora actually started one story, got three pages into it and then felt that it wasn't working. "Closet Monsters" came after that. But when both of us got sidetracked halfway—by homework and real life—we came back to the story, forgetting how it was going to, er, end.

But together we figured out what was really happening to Gina…and what was really in the closet. Oh, yes—both of us got a little scared writing this. Especially when it got late.

CLOSET MONSTERS

by Matthew J. Costello and Nora Claire Costello

❖

Gina spit her foamy toothpaste into the shiny sink. The foamy stuff always looked so gross, like when she got sick. Just looking at it could make her feel sick again.

She wiped her hands on her long flannel nightgown. She grabbed a nearby towel and mashed it into her face.

There! she thought. She stepped off the stool that had her name printed on it. She'd gotten it when she was only two years old. She could barely make out all of the letters anymore. Most of them were worn away.

She stopped at her bedroom door and looked into the room, as she always did. She needed to see how she left it and remember *exactly* how it looked.

That way she could *tell*...

It was important to make sure that everything was the same, that nothing had changed. And that nothing would change during the night when she was sleeping.

The painted rainbows that filled her walls were old now, the colors not so bright. She pounced onto her bed, fluffed the pillow four times, and disappeared into the blankets.

That always felt good.

"Mommy, I'm ready!" She peeked through the covers.

"Teeth brushed?" Her mom started walking up the stairs to Gina's room, a basket of laundry tucked under her arm. Her mom plopped down the laundry at the edge of Gina's bed and sat down next to it. She ruffled Gina's hair, making the brown locks messy. Gina smoothed it down.

Then her mom got up and walked to the closet.

She opened the closet door. She held it open for Gina to inspect. Empty. No dragons. No giant wolves. Just clothes. They had to check the closet every night. Gina made sure of that. Mom said that there weren't any monsters, that they weren't real.

But Gina's fear of monsters was *real.*

"Guess the monsters went home!" her mom said, walking back to the bed.

She tickled Gina, and Gina laughed even though things didn't feel so funny. But Gina was satisfied…for tonight. It didn't feel dangerous tonight.

She kissed her mom and let the hum of the electric heater lull her to sleep.

Gina awoke in the middle of the night. She sat up in bed, her hair sticking to the side of her face from sweat. She often woke up in the night, always sweaty, always wondering.

The door! Mom had closed it, hadn't she?

She looked through the darkness. And the closet door looked open.

It was just a crack, but Mom…she had closed it. Maybe it just popped open? That happened to closet doors sometimes. And no-body knew why.

Gina still sat there in the dark, wishing she could see the closet better.

The house was pretty old. The door just popped open. Gina started to relax. She leaned back. The soft pillow felt good against her neck, still warm.

Mom was right next door, sound asleep. Gina shut her eyes. And the sweet feeling that always came just before sleep swept over her. She was drifting, like floating on a cloud, drifting...

Then she heard it.

It was a creaking sound that she knew could only come from the closet.

Somebody was moving in there. Maybe Mom was in there, look-ing for something.

Gina tilted her head forward on the pillow. She didn't want to move. She peered into the darkness.

"Mom...are you there?"

She waited for an answer. But there was none.

"Mom!" Gina pressed her cheek against the wall. Her mom was on the other side of the wall, in her own bed. She said the word louder, and tears dripped down her cheeks. She pounded and pressed on the wall, as if it might collapse and she could run straight through to her mother's bedroom.

"Please, Mommy...help me..."

In answer, the closet door creaked open a little more.

Gina pounded on the wall. She felt a breeze, but it was a

strangely warm breeze that crawled toward her. She screamed.

And that's when she noticed the smell.

For a moment, Gina froze, her fists stopping their banging on the wall. There was a...smell. It was like—the way the pile of leaves smelled in front of the house when she played in them and her face brushed against the bottom leaves, the wet, soggy leaves.

Her hand kept touching the wall as if that were important.

Was she alone? Why hadn't Mommy heard her? Was she alone in this room, in this house, with—whatever made that creaking noise? With whatever made that smell?

She mouthed the word. "Mommy..." No one could hear it.

She opened her mouth. She thought: If I scream again it will jump out and grab me. It will do that. It will have to do that to keep me quiet.

She didn't know what to do.

But she knew one thing. The smell was stronger. Now it was as if she were buried under that pile of leaves.

She felt herself shaking, crying—quietly.

Something touched her.

Then—a voice—

"Gina, are you okay? Honey, was that you?"

"Mom!"

Then Gina threw herself at her mother, hugging her, moaning into her, over and over.

"Mom, Mom, Mom..."

The next morning Gina's mom said only one thing that showed

that something had happened in the night.

Mom sipped her cup of coffee, standing by the island in the center of the kitchen. Gina was finishing her Fruit Loops.

"Honey, I was wondering—"

Gina looked away from the Cartoon Network to her mother.

"I was wondering whether we should see that man again. You know, when we went and talked to him. About Daddy and—"

Gina shook her head. She spooned in another collection of sweet rainbow O's. She so much wanted to pretend that nothing had happened. But she kept thinking about the empty room, and remembering her crying and pounding on the wall.

With nobody there to help her.

Gina hopped off the tall stool and walked over to the sink. Her toes curled as her feet pressed onto the cold tiles. She dumped the soggy Fruit Loops and pinkish milk into the sink. The soggy circles sat in the drain.

And Gina wanted to flick the little switch that made the sink eat up all the garbage. Mom never let her do that. She said it was too dangerous. But Gina didn't like the loops sitting there, all soggy and fat. She stretched out to the wall where the switch was. She could almost reach—

"Don't touch that!" Her mom turned around and glared into Gina's eyes. "You're going to hurt yourself one of these days. You never listen to me."

Her mom sighed and started fumbling through her purse for the car keys. "Now please get dressed. We're running late. As usual."

❀   ❀   ❀

Gina pushed open the big door to her kindergarten class. All the other kids were already at their tables with their work bins. Gina put her lunch box and coat in her cubby. She looked at the funny little apple sticker on the shelf.

"You're late, Gina." Miss Lane looked up at Gina. Gina lowered her head. Miss Lane wasn't much fun.

"I know."

"Everyone's already started, so get your work bin and take your seat." Some kids were laughing at her. She knew why. Sure, she thought. It was because of her daddy. It was because he *disappeared.* One day he was there, and the next…

She felt them looking at her. She hated all of the kids. She just wanted to scream at them.

He didn't just disappear.

But what would be the point of telling them that?

Two-thirty took forever to come.

But finally it was time to leave. And her mom would come to take her home.

Gina stood at the doorway of the school building, waiting for her mom's Escort to pull up and take her away from this place.

The waiting was bad. She didn't like standing under the overhang with all the other kids, looking down the long driveway. Gina had to think about something that the other kids didn't. She had to go home, have dinner, watch TV, be read to…and go to bed.

Then it would start.

And for some reason, she felt more scared about tonight than she had ever felt before.

Mommy had a word for it.

Routine. It was the same routine each time, getting into her toasty flannel pajamas, brushing her teeth, yelling down to Mom, "I'm ready."

But unlike the other nights, she didn't run into her bed and wait. That didn't seem like a good idea tonight.

"Mom," she called, standing in the hall. "I'm ready!"

Then, more slowly than normal, her mother came up the stairs. Mom had her head turned away, and—for a second—Gina didn't notice anything odd.

Then the light from the bathroom caught the glistening trails on her mother's cheeks.

"You were crying."

Her mom's hand quickly flew up to her eyes and brushed at them.

"No, I wasn't."

Gina didn't say anything more about Mom's lie.

She could guess why Mom was crying.

That was easy.

Her mom smiled as she pulled the blanket up tight against Gina's chin. Gina smiled back.

"You okay, kid?"

Gina nodded. She could lie too.

And all the time, she was thinking, *Why does this night feel dif-*

ferent? Why does it feel so much more dangerous?

Her mother stood up. She went to the closet. She opened it.

"Nothing in here. Everyone's gone home," her mom said. Then she shut the closet door. "Sleep tight."

Gina nodded.

Her mother started to turn away.

"Mom."

She stopped. "What is it?"

Gina could see how tired her mom was, how she was thinking about going downstairs to lie on the couch, or maybe go to bed herself.

"Mommy, can we talk about Daddy?"

Her mom shook her head. "Gina, sweetheart. Not tonight. I'm very tired."

"But I have the same feeling, Mommy. The same exact feeling tonight that I had *that* night."

Now her mother walked back to the bed and sat down.

"Okay. I—I think I know what you're feeling. I don't like living without Daddy. I miss him too. But—"

"It got him, Mom."

Gina's mother brought a hand to her brow and smoothed it. It felt so comforting, this warm, smooth hand patting her, the same way Gina patted her cat, Abu. Before Abu ran away. Back when she still had a cat.

"Daddy's gone, Gina. Sometimes men—husbands, daddies— they do that. He left. Maybe he'll come back, but—but—"

Were there new shiny trails on her mother's cheek? Gina felt bad. Was she making her cry again? She didn't want to do that. But she had to tell her mom. She had to make her understand...

"No," Gina said. "That night I got scared. The closet door—"

Both of them looked over at the closet door.

"—opened. Just a bit. Like it always does. I yelled. Daddy was still up, Mommy. He was downstairs."

The hand kept smoothing Gina's brow. "I know, baby. You told me this. And I'm sure—"

"I yelled. It was late. But Daddy was still up and he came in."

"Shhh—"

"He told me to close my eyes. He told me that this time he was going to scare the closet monsters away. He told me—"

"Gina, Daddy's gone. You have to—"

"He laughed. And he said, 'Gina—I'll scare those monsters away once and for all.' That's what he said and—"

Her mom stood up. The hand was removed. And Gina knew that she had upset her mother.

"It's late, Gina. You've told me this before. I'm sorry you still think about that—that story. But it's late."

Her mother started toward the door.

"Go to sleep. Good night."

"Good night," Gina said. Her mom hadn't understood. No, she couldn't understand what Gina was trying to say.

Gina looked out the window. It was so dark out there, no moonlight at all, and only the one dull streetlight halfway down the block.

She thought that she'd fight to stay awake.

But that was impossible....

Gina woke up in the middle of the night. Did the closet pop open? Was there a noise?

Or maybe it was just as Mom said, just part of the *routine*.

I wake up every night, she thought. *It's what I do.*

But this night she felt something different. It wasn't just a feeling from inside...the one that usually woke her up. This was real.

Something was touching her.

She felt something on her leg. Something was definitely touching her.

Then it went away. And then something touched her higher up, on her back, like a finger tracing a letter.

She tried to scream, not turning around because she knew it would be there, the thing from the closet ready to drag her into the closet and take her away forever.

But she couldn't scream. Her mouth went dry, as if someone were choking her. The scratching on her back became harder, more like digging now. It was going to open her back. It was cutting.

Please, she thought, *make it stop! It hurts.*

The thing wanted her. She couldn't keep it away. She couldn't move, she couldn't speak. She tried to call for her mom, but the sounds wouldn't come.

Gina now remembered the night Daddy came in, as if it were a movie in her head.

And then she knew.

It didn't want Gina. It wanted Mom. Just as it had wanted

Daddy. It would take her mom and then leave Gina all alone. It wanted Gina to bang on the wall so Mommy would come running in, just as she did every night. But tonight it would take Mommy. Then she would be gone. She'd leave Gina alone forever, as Daddy had.

Her back was bleeding. She knew it was. She could tell.

It was just like the way it felt when she fell off her bike and scraped her knee. Gina reached back with her hand to feel the wound. But her elbow knocked against her Rainbow Brite lamp. It crashed to the floor. She didn't care; she had to feel where she hurt.

She rubbed her back trying to stop the blood.

But her back was smooth. There was nothing there. No cuts, no blood. Nothing.

She wondered: if she tried, could she scream? If she tried real hard...

But then Mom would come in, and it would get her.

It scared her, and that made it stronger.

Gina knew that she was only there to make her mom come and be taken away.

She had to get the thing out of her head, out of her closet, and out of her life. She looked toward the closet. She chewed her lip. She tried to speak bravely.

"I'm not scared of you. Neither is Mommy, and Daddy wasn't either." She didn't know if she was talking to nothing, or if something was actually there.

The hall light went on.

"I heard a crash, Gina." Her mom walked into the room. Her mom was here. *But Mom can't be here,* Gina thought. *No, not near the closet, not tonight!*

"The closet…" Gina said. But that was the wrong thing to say.

Her mom looked over at the closet.

"There's nothing there. If I've showed you once, I've showed you a million times." Her mom walked groggily over to the closet. Gina stumbled out of bed, but her blanket clung to her ankles. She took a step. She felt pain. A piece of glass from the lamp cut her foot. She started crying. But she kept running, racing her mom to the closet.

Gina tripped over a roll in her rug, and collapsed just at the bottom of the closet door. She quickly scrambled to her feet and pulled open the door the rest of the way.

And she looked inside.

Gina hoped it would be empty. Just old toys, clothes, darkness.

But it was there.

It was round—like the ball she took to the beach. Except this ball filled the closet, spinning with terrible bumps on it. It didn't look so scary. Not until the bumps started moving around, bubbling, like huge eyes, all puffed up.

It felt as if the ball could see her fear.

She thought: *The ball needs my fear. The eyes need to see me being scared.*

But if she made it appear, could she make it go away?

She raised a hand. There wasn't a lot of time. The closet door was moving as Mom yanked the door open all the way.

Gina took a breath. Then she pushed her hand into the ball.

It sucked at her hand, gripping it, tugging at it. It felt hungry.

But then the ball disappeared.

Her mom pulled open the door completely.

"See? I told you there was nothing there. I'm very proud of you, though, for looking inside by yourself. You've become a brave girl. Now let's clean up your broken lamp and get back to bed."

They shut the door together. Tight.

It might pop open later. But Gina told herself that she'd never be scared of it again.

She walked with her mom back to the broken lamp.

Beth: So you wanna write a story with me?

Brian: Will I get any money?

Beth: Some.

Brian: How much?

Beth: We'll find out later. Want to?

Brian: Okay.

Beth: So what do you wanna write?

Brian: I don't know. What do you wanna write?

Beth: I don't know. What do you wanna write?

Brian: How about a scary middle-school story?

Beth: Yeah, that's a good idea. I used to teach in a middle school. We could do a tale about a frog dissection gone wrong. That'll be scary.

Brian: Nope. Not scary. Dissections are cool. After you cut and pin them open you can take the guts out and put them into your friends' bookbags.

Beth: Okay. No frog dissection. So what are we gonna do? Listen, it wasn't so long ago that you were in middle school. What did you think was scary?

Brian: Band was scary. Scary directors, strange instruments played by creepy kids who knew what they were doing, solos when you least expected them, scary directors, sheet music that looked the same upside down as right side up, scary directors...

Beth: I think we have our story.

Brian: Yeah. I think we do. Pretty cool.

THE MERRY MUSIC OF MADNESS

by Elizabeth Massie and Brian Massie

Twelve-year-old Mark Todd, the new kid, sat in the band room, trying not to look like an idiot. All around him, band members were settling down, waiting for the director, Mr. Shifflett, to come out of his office.

On the floor at Mark's feet was his trumpet case. Mark hoped Mr. Shifflett wouldn't make him play a solo. The band here at Perry Middle School was the best in the state. They always won trophies at festival competitions.

Mark nervously raked his fingers through his brown hair.

And then Mr. Shifflett came into the room. He was tall and thin, with black hair slicked to his head. All the students went instantly quiet. They all smiled at the director. Mark took a deep breath.

No solo, please, he thought.

Mr. Shifflett hopped onto his director's stand, looked the class over, then stared straight at Mark.

"So," the man said. "You're the new boy. And good enough to be in our band? Play your C scale!"

Mark fumbled with his case, got out his trumpet, and stood up. All the students turned to listen to him.

Their grins were huge and toothy.

And creepy.

The horn trembled in Mark's hands, but he began to play.

Immediately, all the students covered their ears. Mr. Shifflett pounded his hand on the podium.

"Stop playing!" he commanded. "Is that a school horn?"

Mark lowered his trumpet and shook his head.

"No wonder, then," the director said. "We play only school instruments here. They have the best sound." The man went to the storage room, unlocked it, then disappeared inside. When he came out, he was holding a shiny trumpet in his hands. He thrust it at Mark. "There," he said. "The instrument makes all the difference."

"But," Mark began. His own trumpet was a fine one. His father had bought it for him on his birthday, and Mark had taken good care of it. There was no way this school trumpet could be better than his.

Mr. Shifflett leaned close to Mark. Mark moved back a step. "But what?"

"But nothing," Mark said. This man was the director of an award-winning band. To argue with him would be stupid.

"Your C scale again," the man said.

Mark glanced down at the trumpet. And his mouth fell open.

It had too many valves.

This trumpet was built wrong. It had five valves instead of three. How was he supposed to play it?

"Can you play or not?" asked the director.

Slowly, Mark held it up to his mouth. He put his fingers where he thought they should go. He blew two notes, then stopped. He didn't know how to play this trumpet.

"It is apparent that you know very little about music," said Mr. Shifflett. "At least, about true music. With my help, maybe you'll learn. Now sit."

Mark sat, feeling lost, feeling angry. Feeling like an idiot.

Looking at the girl next to him, Mark saw that her flute was not like any he'd seen before. It had two rows of holes instead of one. Mark peered around the room, hoping Mr. Shifflett didn't catch him looking. All the instruments were strange. Some were lopsided, some too small, others too large.

What is going on here? Mark thought.

But then the class began to play. In a single, smooth motion, Mr. Shifflett raised his hands and the students raised their instruments. The music that filled the room was happy, beautiful, and perfect.

And it made Mark feel as if he were going to throw up.

The cafeteria was crowded. Not knowing anyone, Mark sat near two boys who were also in the band. He hoped they would talk with him, but they didn't. And so, Mark spoke first.

"Is there something in the band room that makes you feel sick?" Mark asked.

One of the boys glanced at Mark and frowned. "No. Why?'

Mark shrugged. "I don't know."

"Band makes us feel great," said the second boy.

Mark took a breath. "Okay," he said. "But those instruments sure are strange, don't you think?"

The first boy frowned. "What are you saying?"

"They're built wrong. The trumpets have too many valves. The tubas' bells are oval, not round, and the—"

Suddenly, the boy grabbed Mark's shirt collar. His lips pulled back into a snarl. "Don't you ever criticize the band!"

"Uh," said Mark. "I just think it's weird that..." And then he stopped talking. He looked behind him. Mr. Shifflett stood there, holding a bagged lunch.

"Behaving yourselves?" the man asked.

"Oh, sure, Mr. Shifflett, you bet," said the boy who'd grabbed him. He was smiling again, a stupid ear-to-ear grin.

"Good, then," Mr. Shifflett said. He reached out a hand and put it on Mark's shoulder. The touch was clammy.

And as Mr. Shifflett walked away, it looked to Mark as if the man's lunch bag was *glowing*.

A week came and went. Mark's fingers couldn't make sense of the five-valve trumpet. Every day in band class, he felt fine until the students began to play. Then his stomach would cramp and his head would spin. It was weird.

Mark was digging in his locker one morning when someone nudged him in the back. He looked around. Behind him stood a boy from band, John Winthrop. The boy held a bright green bookbag by the straps.

John spoke in a whisper. "I'm not like the others. I don't think you are either."

"Huh?" said Mark.

"I've been in band since the beginning of this year. It still makes me sick. But he hasn't been able to take me."

Mark shut his locker door. "Take you?"

"Mr. Shifflett has bad power. But I'm too strong for him. I think you're strong too."

"Wait a minute—"

"I'm quitting before he figures out that I know about him. You should quit, too, Mark."

"John," began Mark, but John spun around, green bookbag whipping the air. He vanished into the crowd of students.

"Power?" Mark said to himself. "That's crazy."

But the rest of the day, all Mark could think about was the fear he'd seen in John's eyes, the fear he'd heard in John's voice.

"Look," Mark's mother consoled. "He's the director of the number-one band in the state. He has high expectations of his students. You've been in the band for only a week. Be patient."

Mark stood in the kitchen doorway as his mother put away dishes.

"He gives me the creeps," Mark said.

"In third grade, Mrs. Wampler gave you the creeps too."

"But I feel like I am going to throw up whenever we play. After class I have to go outside to keep from passing out."

"It's probably nerves, Mark. As I said, be patient."

"John Winthrop quit yesterday," said Mark. "Mr. Shifflett didn't seem to mind. He just said, 'We can get on without John.' So you see, Mom, they can get on without me, too."

Mark's mother slammed down a glass and looked at her son. "Stop whining! You aren't quitting! Now go do your homework!"

Mark went to his room and played his own trumpet. He felt like crying. But at least his own instrument didn't make him sick.

The next day, Mark tried not to think about band. Maybe it really was just nerves.

And maybe he was the man in the moon.

As he walked into history class, the teacher, Miss King, pointed to the overflowing trash can. "Mark, would you empty this in the Dumpster?"

Mark picked up the can and headed out the door.

The Dumpster was outside the band room. The air was cold, but Mark could do this quickly. He threw the can up and over the side of the container, then climbed up to empty the contents. The smell was atrocious. He wrinkled his nose and began to shake out the can's contents. Then he noticed something bright green beneath some old spiral notebooks. With his foot, he pushed the notebooks aside.

It was a bright green bookbag. A bookbag with dried drops of blood and the initials JRW.

"John Winthrop!" Mark gasped.

Mark jumped back, grabbed the trash can, and ran back to class.

After history, he knew what he had to do. He had to tell an adult. Someone had to know.

His throat dry and his hands sweating, he went to the office.

Inside, the principal was talking quietly with a woman. Mark sat on a chair to wait. He couldn't help but overhear the principal's final words to the woman.

"Mrs. Winthrop, thank you for coming in. Let us know if you hear any more."

Mrs. Winthrop!

Mark jumped from his chair and followed the woman into the hall.

"Excuse me!"

The woman looked at Mark. Her eyes were red, as if she had been crying. "Yes?"

"Has something happened to John?"

The woman sniffed. "Why, yes. He ran away. I got a note from him in the mail last night."

"He ran away?"

"Yes, why do you ask?"

Mark thought about the bookbag in the Dumpster. Maybe John had just thrown it there himself. Maybe he'd cut his finger on the sharp Dumpster edge. *Maybe I'm just losing my mind,* he thought.

"Just wondering," said Mark. "I'm sorry he ran away."

Mrs. Winthrop nodded, wiping her eyes.

Mark hurried to band so he wouldn't get a tardy slip.

Everyone in band was excited. Mr. Shifflett was going to announce who had solos for the concert.

Mark sat next to the flute player, Janice Monroe, and waited as

Mr. Shifflett stapled a sheet to the bulletin board. Mark could feel the students around him smiling like painted puppets. It made his skin crawl.

"I'm so proud of my band," said Mr. Shifflett, waving his thin hand in the air. "Just listening to you makes me feel young and alive! Come now, and see our soloists!"

Permission granted, all the students rushed forward to the bulletin board. Even though he knew he wouldn't be on the list, Mark still got up to see.

Suddenly, the lights went out in the classroom. The second hand on the wall clock stopped. Someone bumped into Mark, knocking him down.

"Ouch!" Mark grunted as he hit the floor on his back.

"Don't panic, students," said Mr. Shifflett. "The electricity's gone off. It'll be back on in a second."

But a second was all Mark needed. As he glanced up from the floor, he saw the eyes of the students near him. They were standing with their backs to the windows.

Mark could see the light from the windows, shining out through the students' eyes. Pouring through their heads and out their eyes like car headlights, like jack-o'-lantern eyes with candles behind them. As if they had no brains to block the light.

As if they had no souls!

Mark's hand flew to his mouth. He bit his tongue to keep from crying out. He scrambled to his feet, his heart pounding. He glanced away from the students to the base of the storage room door.

And from beneath the door, he could see an eerie, flickering

blue glow. A glow like the one Mark thought he'd seen in Mr. Shifflett's lunch bag.

Then the lights came back on and everyone sat down to practice for the concert. As though nothing at all was wrong.

Mark skipped lunch and hid in the boys' bathroom. No one was in the band room during this period. Now was the only time Mark could go in there without being seen.

John Winthrop had said, "He hasn't been able to take me." He had been talking about Mr. Shifflett, of course. And Mark was going to find out what was going on.

Mark crept down the hall to the band room. He'd never been so scared in his life. Taking a deep breath, he opened the door and went inside.

It was empty, except for the instruments leaning against chairs. Mark tiptoed to the storage room door. It was locked.

He hurried to the band room office. The door opened easily. Inside, Mark found a small desk. There was no key on top. He opened the top desk drawer, his hands trembling. There, in a tray, was a single key on a ring.

Taking the key, Mark went out into the band room again. The instruments still leaned against the chairs, as silent as band students waiting for Mr. Shifflett's directions.

Mark shivered.

He went to the storage room and tried the key. It clicked. The knob turned.

Mark pushed open the door and went inside.

It was the blue glow that caught his attention first. On the back wall, on shelves that held several flutes and clarinets, was a row of glass jars. His pulse pounding in his neck, Mark eased the door shut, then walked over to the jars. Each one glowed like a tiny blue lantern. And each one had a little label on it.

One label read JANICE MONROE.

He read all the labels. Each jar had the name of a band student on it.

And then he saw an empty jar. It read MARK TODD.

Suddenly he heard a thumping in the corner. He grabbed a flute, held it up, then inched over to where he'd heard the sound. It was hard to see in the shadows. He squinted. There was a form sitting in the corner.

"Who is that?" Mark demanded.

There was a muffled cry.

Mark leaned closer. "John!"

John Winthrop was in the corner, his mouth gagged, his arms and legs tied together.

Mark dropped to his knees and worked the gag from John's mouth. When the gag was loose, John said, "Hurry! We can't let Mr. Shifflett find us!"

Mark loosened the ropes from John's arms and legs. As John stood up, Mark asked, "Why did he put you in here? What are those jars?"

"Mr. Shifflett makes all the instruments for the band. They suck the souls out of the people that play them. Mr. Shifflett keeps the souls in the jars. He carries one with him all the time. I don't know why he needs them, but he does. When I quit, he knew that I knew. He put me in here yesterday!"

"The instruments!" said Mark. "That's why the music makes me feel sick!"

"Yes," said John. "And, like me, you've been strong enough to resist them. But we have to get out of here now, before—"

The storage room door slammed open. There, with his eyes flashing, stood Mr. Shifflett.

"Before what, boy?" he shouted.

John stumbled backward. Mark held the flute out in front of him. He had to stand up to the man. Whatever it took.

"Before what?" repeated Mr. Shifflett. He stepped into the storage room. Mark could see the glowing lunch bag in his hand.

"How can you do this to kids?" Mark demanded.

Mr. Shifflett tilted his head. "I do it because I can. There's nothing you can do to stop me."

"Oh, no?" cried Mark. He leaned over to the shelf and with a swipe of his arm sent ten jars smashing to the floor.

Mr. Shifflett's eyes went huge and dark. He shouted, "Don't do that!" and he lunged for Mark. Mark jumped out of his reach and knocked more jars off the shelf.

"Stop it!" shouted Mr. Shifflett. The man's hair began to turn white. His face sank in on itself, his skin wrinkling.

"Mark, get them all!" said John.

Mr. Shifflett ran for Mark again and slammed the boy against the wall. The flute fell from Mark's hands. Mark could feel the man's bones shrinking and aging though the softening muscle. The man groaned in pain. Mark tried to jerk away, but Mr. Shifflett held on tight.

"John, smash them!" shouted Mark.

John grabbed the flute Mark had dropped and hurled it at the last of the jars. They fell like bowling pins and rolled from the shelf.

"No!" screamed Mr. Shifflett.

The jars hit the floor, exploding into glass shards and blue glow.

Mr. Shifflett went limp. Mark jumped up and stared as Mr. Shifflett's body changed from old man to older man to a dry, papery mummy.

"What happened?" John whispered.

"I guess," Mark said softly, "I guess the souls kept him young. He must have been a band director for a long, long time."

"I guess," said John.

"What about the souls now?" Mark asked. He turned and looked at the jars. And what he saw was the most amazing thing of all. The glows had risen from the broken glass like a cloud of blue fireflies. They flew around one another, making patterns in the air, as if they were happy to be free. And then they all darted out of the storage room.

"I think they're going back to their owners," said John.

Mark smiled a little smile. "I think you're right." Then Mark saw the glowing lunch bag, still gripped in Mr. Shifflett's skeletal fingers. Mark picked it up, opened the bag, and dropped the jar to the floor. As it shattered, the single glow flew into the air and shot out of the storage room.

"Who was that?" asked John.

"It doesn't matter," said Mark. "It's gone back home."

The two boys went out into the band room. They stopped and looked at the instruments. The five-valved trumpet. The oval-belled tuba. The strange flutes, drums, and baritones.

John lifted one of the music stands. He swung hard, driving it into the bell of the nearest tuba. The tuba caved in.

Laughing, Mark picked up a trumpet and broke off all five keys. Then he crushed it over a chair. "They'll probably kick me out of band for this!" he said.

John swung his makeshift hammer into another tuba.

When their work was done, they went out of the band room to face the music.

Joseph R. Tem: When I was in foster care, I had a dream every night about an alligator. Then I had other dreams when I was adopted. I don't know why. Dreams just happen.

Then we wrote this story.

Melanie Tem: Actually, there were a couple of other steps in this collaborative process.

Joe recounted his dreams with the mixture of awe and matter-of-factness—*of course this is real*—with which a reader responds to a good story. Thinking about my son's dreams made me think about what's scary and what's friendly—it touched and fascinated me, for instance, that at first the hearts were scarier than the alligator—and how the same image can change from one to the other depending on what we bring to it.

But I guess, basically, I don't know why either. Dreams just happen. So do stories.

Melanie Tem   *Joseph R. Tem*

HOUSE FULL
OF HEARTS

by Melanie Tem and Joseph R. Tem

Something big and pink and squishy was pushing open Danny's bedroom door.

It was the middle of the night, and Danny was the only one awake. He was pretty used to that. In every house he'd ever lived in he knew things nobody else did, because he was awake when nobody else was.

A lot of times he used to get up and wander around at night, even outside. He used to wake up other people, other kids, so he could tell them what he'd discovered about the nighttime house, but they never believed him. They thought he was just being mean, waking them up. It got him in a lot of trouble.

Once Mom and Dad said that was the reason he had to go live someplace else, because he wouldn't stay in bed at night.

Danny really didn't want to get in trouble in *this* family. Besides, if you stayed in your bed at night, at least the monster had to come to you.

Which was what was happening right now. Danny lay still and opened his eyes wide. He'd learned that there was no point in closing your eyes, because then you just couldn't see what was coming. He'd also learned that hiding under the covers didn't do any good, because scary stuff burrowed underneath and got you anyway. Scary stuff could get you anywhere, anytime it felt like it, and the world was full of scary stuff.

If he rolled down into the crack between his bed and wall, the alligator that lived under the bed would eat him. That alligator had really long jaws.

Used to be, the alligator ate him every night because he wouldn't stay in bed. He'd been a lot more scared of staying in bed and falling asleep than of the alligator. Every night the alligator ate him with its long jaws full of long teeth, and every morning it spat him up again. Danny used to sort of daydream about what it would be like if someday the alligator just refused to let him go.

Actually, he didn't know if the alligator had come with him to this house or not. He hadn't seen it since he'd been here. But *every* house, *every* family, had monsters in it, and he'd been waiting to see what ones lived in *this* one. Now he guessed he was about to find out.

The pink squishy thing squeezed more of itself inside his room. Danny never would have thought of pink for the color of a monster. But he should have known by now that anything could be scary if it wanted to be.

This thing was really big, a lot bigger than the door. At first that made him feel a little safer—maybe it couldn't fit through. But then he realized it was so soft that it could fit anywhere just by changing its shape, which wouldn't change what it was.

He didn't know what it was. He'd never seen anything like it before. But it was mean, he could tell, and it was after him. He didn't know why, but sooner or later every monster in every house always came after him.

All of a sudden that made him furious. It wasn't fair. He reached out and knocked a bunch of stuff off the shelves. He grabbed his remote control car and threw it as hard as he could at the pink thing. It banged against the wall. The monster was so huge that Danny didn't know how he could have missed.

He waited for somebody to come in to see what all the noise was about and tell him to settle down. It was way past bedtime.

But nobody came, and he got over being mad.

Danny was good at getting mad; he'd practiced. One time he'd scratched a dad's fancy car with a nail, all the way along both sides. One time he'd bitten a mom's shoulder while she was holding him in her lap. If he got mad enough, he could get himself sent away. Usually what they said was that they couldn't be the kind of parents he needed, but Danny always knew exactly what he'd done.

He didn't want to leave *this* family. But if their monsters turned out to be scary enough, he might.

With a squeaky, squishy noise the monster pushed Danny's door all the way open. It completely filled up the doorway, and Danny knew that the part of the monster you could see was always a lot smaller than the part you couldn't see.

The hall light looked pink and blurry through the pink monster. It must be blocking the bathroom door, too. Anyone who got up to go to the bathroom would run right into it. But no mom or dad ever knew they had monsters living in their house, and all of them did. Danny was the only one who knew.

Besides oozing farther and farther toward him, the pink thing was moving in and out, in and out. It was shiny as if it were wet, and it glistened when it moved. There was a thumping, just as when a car went by with the stereo up so loud all you could hear was the beat. Not even hear it, really, but feel it in your bones and teeth. His whole room, probably the whole house, probably the whole city and the whole country and the whole *world* vibrated. It made his body itch from the inside. He curled up. His heart was beating like that, too, *tha-thump, tha-thump.*

The pink monster was all the way to his dresser now. It dripped into the drawer he'd left half-open this morning when he was hunting for the caterpillar to take to school—he never had found it, so maybe it had turned into a butterfly and flown away. Danny wasn't sure he believed that caterpillars did that, but that's what everybody said. Now he'd have to put all his socks and underwear in the laundry, and they'd ask why and he'd say, "To get the monster slime off." They'd smile and say uh-huh, but they'd think it was really because of the caterpillar, which they probably knew about.

The monster oozed over his model train tracks. Now the wheels wouldn't turn right. It slid over his comic books like chewing gum, sticking the pages together. It knocked over the peanut butter jar full of grass and dirt where he'd put a cricket a long time ago, and then hadn't been able to find it. When the jar tipped over and rolled across the floor, he swore he heard chirping. He didn't think he believed that crickets chirped with their legs, either.

Maybe there'd be a slime trail or footprints on his rug in the morning. Actually, though, Danny knew better than that. Monsters never left evidence that they'd been there, except in your mind.

The slimy thing touched his bare back where his pajama top had pulled up, and Danny yelped. It messed with his hair like somebody running fingers through it. It made a disgusting damp spot on his cheek like a kiss. Danny said, "Yuck!"

Then it started to wrap him up as if he were a baby and needed to be held. He was not a baby. It was all warm and sticky, and he sank right into it like quicksand. It was beating, *tha-thump*. Danny could hardly breathe.

With a *pop* he got himself out. He pushed away and scooted to the edge of the bed and rolled on over, wedged himself between the bed and the wall and dropped all the way down. The sheets and blankets were bunched up as protection against the alligator and they caught him like a circus net, so he had to tug at them and wriggle to get through.

The alligator was asleep under the bed. Danny saw it, but he also saw the pink feet of the monster—foot, actually, one pointy foot—through the fringe of his Batman bedspread. Alligators slept with their eyes open, like dragons. This alligator had blue eyes, sometimes purple. As Danny eased himself right past it, practically brushing against its rubbery hide, he expected it to wake up and close its eyes and eat him. But it didn't. It was snoring. Danny almost grinned.

He sneaked past the alligator, and past the cowboy boots he'd got for the first birthday he'd had in this family, and past a heap of crumpled-up homework, mostly penmanship. When he got to the

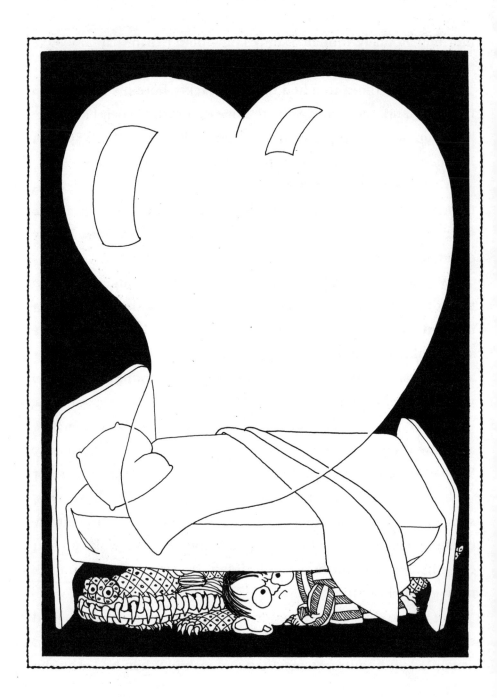

end of the bed, he stuck out his hand and moved the blue fringe of the bedspread apart. There was space in his doorway where the monster had come into the room. Not much space, but some.

Everybody said Danny was a good runner. He edged out from under the bed. He squatted against the wall under the window, got himself ready, and sprang.

The pink thing didn't even try to stop him. In fact, it shrank against the other side of the door frame and changed its shape to let him by. Expecting a fight, Danny had been charging harder and faster than he needed to, and so he tumbled out into the hall.

He lay there for a minute to catch his breath. Then he sat up and looked back. He could see all of the pink monster now, where it perched on his bed looking kind of sad and sorry.

It was a giant heart, like a valentine, and it was beating gently, *tha-thump, tha-thump.* Danny had the feeling that he'd just barely escaped something awful, and also that he'd given up something nice.

Now he couldn't go back in his room for the rest of the night. Because of the monster, he'd have to find someplace else to sleep, or just to pass the time. He'd done that before, lots of times. There was something about being the only one awake in the middle of the night that made Danny feel powerful. It also made him feel lonely.

He hesitated outside his parents' room. When you had a bad dream you were supposed to go crawl in bed with your parents so you could feel safe and go back to sleep. He'd never done that, even though they said he could. The heart monster wasn't a dream, but maybe he'd see if they'd let him get in bed with them anyway and not get mad at him for waking them up.

He stood just outside their door and peered in. He didn't think he ought to just go on in, because he wasn't sure he'd be welcome. He ought to be invited. If they really meant what they'd said, they'd know he was there and invite him in.

But they were sound asleep. And in between them in the big bed was a red heart, longer and fatter than both of them and taking almost all the covers.

Danny caught his breath and clapped a hand over his mouth to keep himself quiet. He stared at the heart monster in his parents' bed. He could swear it stared back at him even though it didn't have any eyes. Then he turned around and tiptoed away.

He started down the hall toward the kitchen. If he got caught, he could just say he was hungry. Now that he thought of it, he was.

The kitchen was full of monster hearts. Danny counted eight from where he hid behind the pantry cupboard. The hearts were all mushed together, so he couldn't really tell which was which. Some of them were pink. Some of them were bright red or dark red. At least one of them was a sort of maroon color. They were all glistening. They were all thumping, so it sounded like drum music from the kitchen radio. On top they had humps, like shoulders without heads, and they balanced on points at the bottom.

They were all gathered around the stove and the table as if they wanted something to eat. Danny was sure they were waiting for him. Well, he was not going to be their midnight snack. He backed away.

Into something squishy and moist and *tha-thump*ing against his back. It was a lot bigger than he was, and so much stronger that he felt stupid trying to fight it, but he fought anyway. It didn't have arms, but it put its whole soft self around him and wouldn't let him go.

He felt as though he were swimming in a giant heart-shaped jar of strawberry jelly. His whole body went in and out, in and out, when the heart did. His own heart was thumping fast and hard, and now he couldn't tell whether the heartbeat that filled the house belonged to him or to the monster.

Danny punched. He kicked. He even bit into the slimy red mass, and it didn't taste as bad as he had thought it would. He twisted. The harder he struggled, the more the heart closed in. It didn't hold him tight. It didn't hurt him. But it was all over him, all around him, and he couldn't get loose.

After a while Danny quit fighting. He wasn't giving up. He was resting and trying to figure out what to do next. The heart monster was like a huge red pillow, and he didn't know if he was lying on it or sitting on it or kneeling or even standing. It was really soft. The heartbeat was like his own heartbeat, and it kind of calmed him down. It was comfortable here. He felt himself relaxing. That was not a good idea.

Danny moved.

Hearts couldn't have laps. Monsters couldn't either. But now he was slipping off the heart monster's big soft lap, and he didn't want to. The monster pulled away from him, as if Danny had hurt its feelings, and then he was free of it.

Suddenly, he found himself on top of the dining room table,

which was so weird that he laughed out loud. Hearts were everywhere. The bay window was stuffed with them, like balloons, all different shades of pink and red and purple. In every chair there was a heart, like a big family ready for dinner. Some of them drooped over the seats like fat people. Some reached way up almost to the ceiling.

Danny made a mean face at the fire-engine red heart in his chair. Last Easter, Grampa had sat in Danny's chair, and that had made Danny so mad that he'd thrown a tantrum and refused to come to the table. Nobody had understood what was the matter and he'd been afraid to say.

The red heart wouldn't budge, so Danny went and plopped himself down on top of it. It was soft and warm under him, and it wiggled to fit his body. There was plenty of room for both of them in Danny's chair. That was kind of fun.

Then he got down and went exploring through the house. The whole entire house was full of hearts. Hearts hung from the ceiling like chandeliers, like round cobwebs. Every door had turned into a heart. Danny opened and shut the heart-doors and they all still worked, but they moved funny and made squishy sounds.

The front yard and the backyard and the steps were covered with hearts. They looked like snowballs somebody had dipped in red food coloring—some a lot, and some a little. The bathtub was about to overflow with what looked like bubble bath but was really hearts. Bookshelves had hearts instead of books, plants had sprouted fat new red and purple heart-shaped leaves. All of the hearts *tha-thump*ed. The whole house moved gently and steadily in and out, in and out. Danny was getting sleepy.

It was almost morning. That was okay, because tomorrow wasn't a school day and he could sleep as late as he wanted. He could always sleep better in the daylight.

Getting through the hearts in the hall wasn't hard if he just let himself be carried along. They didn't try to keep him out of his room; in fact, they invited him in.

His bed had turned into one huge beating heart, like a waterbed. To avoid the alligator, not wanting it to eat him ever again, Danny took a running leap from the doorway and landed with a *plump* in the middle of his heart monster, which *tha-thump*ed as if it were glad to see him. He sank in and got scared, but he bounced right back up again.

Maybe with this kind of bed, he could finally sleep at night. Maybe the heart monster would protect him from all the other monsters in the house. He remembered to relax. He snuggled down into the monster and fell asleep.

Collaborating, we have discovered, is not a very easy thing to do, but it certainly was a lot of fun.

One rainy weekend afternoon—between swimming lessons, soccer games, karate class, and Super Nintendo bouts with friends—we sat down in Rick's ("Pops'") office for a brainstorming session.

And brainstorm we did.

We came up with quite a few cool ideas, but ultimately we decided to go with the UFO abduction idea. (We're not giving anything away here, because you find that out in the first scene.)

Maybe because we had three minds working on it, instead of the usual one, generating a story line was relatively easy. The only problem we encountered happened after we had our basic "story" mapped out. We realized that the original ending, as suggested by seven-year-old Matti, was a little too graphic and gruesome for this anthology, so we toned things down—a little.

With input from the kids, "Pops" wrote the first draft in two days. We then printed it out, read it, commented upon it, and made some changes (mostly to fit the word count limit).

The finished result will—hopefully—raise a few goose bumps.

We know it did for us!

Jesse Hautala

Rick Hautala

Matti Hautala

ABDUCTION

by Rick Hautala, Jesse Hautala, and Matti Hautala

"So when did this headache start?"

Nick Hansen rubbed his forehead just above his left eyebrow as he stared at his mother. She was looking at him over her shoulder as she stood at the kitchen sink and scraped their breakfast plates. The high, whining sound of the garbage disposal jacked Nick's headache up another notch.

"I'm not sure," he said, wincing as the needle-sharp pain jabbed behind his left eye. "Sometime during the night, I guess."

Nick thought he caught a funny glint in his mother's eyes when she turned and walked over to where he was sitting. Smiling tightly, she knelt down in front of him and gripped his shoulders.

"You guess?"

Nick shrugged as he nibbled on his lower lip for a second. He shifted uneasily beneath his mother's touch and her steady gaze.

"I've—I think I might've had it for the last couple of days or so."

"Just the last couple of days?"

The expression of genuine concern in his mother's eyes made him feel a tiny bit better, but Nick also wasn't so sure he wanted his mother to be babying him like this. The truth was, he'd been having bad headaches for a couple of weeks now. He hadn't told his mom or his dad about them. After all, he had just turned thirteen! He wasn't going to start acting like a baby about a few headaches.

On the other hand, what if he had a brain tumor? Or maybe something else...maybe something worse!

What could possibly be worse than a brain tumor? Nick wondered. At the same time, he saw that this was exactly the problem: He was always *imagining* too darned much, and it was driving him crazy.

"Yeah," he finally said, finding it difficult to look his mother straight in the eyes. "And I haven't been sleeping so good lately, either."

"So *well*," his mother corrected him "You haven't been sleeping so *well* lately."

"Whatever," Nick replied, his voice almost a whisper.

He glanced at the kitchen clock and tried to wriggle away from his mother, but she held him in check.

"So tell me, Nicky. What is it really?"

His mother stared at him with a hard, penetrating look.

Nick hated the way his parents—especially his mom—seemed to be able to see right through him. He wanted to say something about being late for school, but the worry that was bubbling up inside him was getting stronger. The worry was harder to take than the sharp pain behind his left eye.

"Come on, Nicky. You know you can tell me. What are you worried about now?"

"I was just thinking...what if...what if it's—"

He stopped himself and clamped his teeth together, thinking

that he couldn't tell her what he was afraid of. His parents were already worried enough about him as it was. Last year, they had even talked about having him see a *therapist*. He was pretty sure he didn't need that, but it did bother him how he seemed to worry so much…about everything!

"What if it's *what?*" his mother prodded him. He noticed that her grip on his shoulders had tightened.

"UFOs," he finally said, so low he hardly heard himself speak.

"What—?" his mother said, her grip tightening until it almost hurt.

Nick looked at her, his lower lip trembling.

"I was reading a book…about UFOs…and I was afraid that…maybe I've been abducted."

One side of his mother's mouth twitched into a tight smile before she nodded and said, "Abducted?"

"Yeah," Nick said. "I was just…you know, thinking that maybe I…that they…aliens might be kidnapping me…at night…and…and doing things—experiments—on me."

His mother's half-smile quickly melted. Nick couldn't help but see the worry in her eyes. He cringed, waiting for her to say what she had said to him so many times before: *You can't let your imagination get too carried away, Nicky. It's just not healthy.*

His mother finally let go of his shoulders and stood up.

"You'd better get going," she said, her voice sounding tight and dry. "You don't want to be late for school."

"Did you ever think that maybe you really *are* crazy?"

"Oh, thanks a lot!"

As usual, Nick and his best friend, Denny, were late for class. They were talking breathlessly as they hurried down the empty corridor. The door to Mrs. Wilson's room was already shut. It looked as if they were going to have detention this afternoon.

"C'mon, Nick. You know I don't mean it!"

"Yeah, but..."

"You and your '*yeah, buts*,'" Denny said, smirking slightly as they stopped outside the classroom door. "You know, maybe you *do* read too much of that science fiction stuff. It might be warping your brain."

Nick shook his head. Nobody believed him, not even Denny. As he opened the door, a sudden jab lanced behind his left eye. The pain was sharp enough to make him cry out. Denny looked at him, confused, but it was too late to say anything. Twitters of laughter filled the room as they entered the classroom.

In the few seconds it took Nick to walk to his desk, the vision in his left eye got so blurry he almost lost his balance. No matter where he looked, everything he saw was surrounded by halos of shifting white light.

"Well, well..."

Mrs. Wilson's voice cut through Nick's surge of panic. "I see that you two have finally decided to grace us with your presence."

Mrs. Wilson's arms were folded across her chest as she shifted her gaze back and forth between Nick and Denny. Then she cleared her throat.

Turning back to the blackboard, she said casually over her

shoulder, "I assume you boys know where to be at two-forty-five this afternoon."

That night was much worse than the night before.

Nick tried to force himself to drift off to sleep. It was like trying *not* to think about something. He just couldn't do it.

He picked up a paperback on his nightstand and began to read. It was another book about UFOs. He read only a few pages before it began again.

A slight throb of pain jabbed him behind his left eye, but it wasn't ever strong enough to bother him. He was just happy that he didn't see any more shimmering halos of light wherever he looked.

What *did* have Nick worried was what he saw in the bathroom mirror while brushing his teeth before bed. At first, he hardly noticed. But as he stared at his reflection, Nick discovered a thin white line on the upper inside of his left eyebrow, just beneath the dark hairs.

A cold surge of panic filled him. He leaned close to the mirror and traced the line with his forefinger. It looked like a faint scar that had healed long ago.

Nearly frantic with fear, Nick called out to his mother. But when she came into the bathroom to check on him, he just stared at her. Nick knew exactly what she'd say: *You can't let your imagination get too carried away. It's just not healthy.*

Trembling inside, Nick said nothing about the scar. He simply kissed his mother good night and hurried off to bed.

But he knew that sleep wouldn't come easily.

Worry and fear about that scar on his eyebrow kept Nick awake. Could it be connected to the pain behind his left eye? Could it be evidence of his abduction—by aliens in a UFO?

Then he heard them. The noises.

They came from above him—from the attic. It sounded as though someone was moving around up there—not walking, just moving. It wasn't exactly footsteps that he heard.

Nick lay perfectly still in his bed. He held his breath and strained to listen.

The noises were there, all right, sounding like something soft and spongy being dragged across the floor. A sick shiver came over him. He wanted to call his mother. But when he opened his mouth, no sound came out. He simply stayed in bed, listening to the strange noises in the attic, wondering what they were.

Nick never knew when—or if—he fell asleep. By the time morning light was glowing though his drawn window shades, the pain behind his left eye had returned.

Lying in bed, Nick listened to his mother moving about downstairs in the kitchen as she prepared breakfast. After he heard his father leave for work, Nick called her up to his bedroom and told her that he was too sick to go to school today. Once she was convinced that he wasn't faking it—to avoid a test or something that he hadn't studied for—she gave him two aspirin and told him to stay in bed and try to get some sleep.

Sometime later, a gentle knocking sound awoke Nick.

He wedged his eyes open and braced himself for the usual jolt of pain. But there was none. He was amazed to find that he actually felt better…almost perfect, in fact!

Maybe the aspirin really did the trick! he thought as he lay there, staring up at his bedroom ceiling and wondering why he had awakened so suddenly.

Then, from downstairs, the knocking sound came again. It was followed by the hushed scuff of his mother's footsteps, moving quickly to the front door.

Nick tensed and sat up in bed as he stared at his bedroom door. He was suddenly fearful that he might be dreaming all of this, and that someone—or some*thing*—was going to rush into his room.

When that didn't happen, he swung his feet to the floor. He tiptoed out into the hallway and squatted on the top step of the staircase. Many times before, he had crouched here to listen to his parents talk. Now he strained to hear what the people at the door were saying to his mother. But all he could make out was a soft, indistinct buzzing of voices.

Once again, his suspicions were up, and questions flooded his mind.

Who was down there, talking to his mother?

And why were they being so quiet?

Was it because they didn't want him to hear?

Nick debated whether or not he should sneak downstairs and see who was there. But before he could do anything, the voices stopped. Next he heard the front door close.

Nick's first reaction was to go back to his bedroom before his mother found him out of bed. But then, almost without thinking, he raced to his parents' bedroom and looked out their window. He almost screamed when he saw two men walking toward the car that was parked down by the road. Both of them were exactly the same height, and both wore long black coats. Dark, wide-brimmed hats were pulled down on both of their heads, almost to their eyebrows. They were also wearing sunglasses. What little Nick could see of their faces looked pale, their skin almost transparent.

The mere sight of these two men in black frightened Nick, but seeing them also made him feel...funny, somehow...as though he almost recognized them.

Have I seen them before? he wondered.

Nick watched as the men got into the car and drove away. For a long time he crouched there by his parents' bedroom window, staring down the street where the men's car had disappeared. It was only when he heard his mother's footsteps on the stairs that he scooted back to his room and got into bed.

"Are you feeling any better?" his mother asked when she poked her head into his bedroom.

Nick wanted to ask her who the men at the door were, but something inside warned him not to let her know that he had seen them—and that he might have seen them before...someplace...if he could only remember...

"Well, now I *know* you're crazy," Denny said later that day as he followed Nick up the narrow stairs and into the attic. The air was stale and dusty, and it made the boys cough.

"I just want to check it out," Nick said, keeping his voice low, even though he knew he didn't have to. His father was still at work, and his mother had gone to the supermarket and wouldn't be back for at least another hour.

"Last night...there were noises. I heard them—strange noises—and they were coming from up here."

"You think this is where the aliens are taking you, huh?" Denny asked.

Nick heard the mocking tone in his friend's voice, but he chose to ignore it. With determination, he walked straight to the middle of the attic floor and looked around.

All his life, he realized, he had been afraid to come up here alone. The attic was dim and dusty, crammed with accumulated junk that Nick couldn't imagine all belonged to his parents. There were piles of old clothes, numerous boxes tied shut with brown string, stacks of old magazines and books, and lots of worn-out, old-fashioned furniture. At the far end of the attic was a large built-in closet, and it was on this that Nick focused his gaze.

"D'you see that?" Nick asked Denny, pointing at the closet. Denny glanced at the closet a moment, then looked back at Nick. Denny shrugged, unimpressed.

"So what, it's a closet!"

Nick covered his mouth with his fist and nodded. He always knew that the closet was up here, but until now he had never thought much about it. Now he realized that he had never looked in that closet—never in all his life. A current of fear played like electricity up his spine as he took a few steps closer to it.

He could see that the door was locked. There was a metal hasp with a small safety lock just above the doorknob.

"Why do you think it's locked?" Nick asked, turning to face Denny.

"Maybe because your parents don't want you fooling around in there."

Nick frowned suspiciously, then took a deep breath and approached the door. Feeling oddly detached, he watched as his hand reached out and took hold of the lock. It was cold to the touch and sent a vibrating chill up Nick's arm.

"Look, Nick," Denny said. "I don't know how to say this without sounding mean or something, but you're kinda creeping me out."

"I just want to see what's inside here," Nick said, hearing the strangled sound of his own voice.

Gritting his teeth, he gave the lock a sudden downward yank. The old, dry wood of the doorframe splintered, and the lock pulled free. Nick's whole body was trembling as he turned the doorknob and swung open the door.

A thick, vibrating wall of darkness surrounded Nick.

He felt lost in the darkness…drifting like a wind-tossed feather in a black, limitless void. Then, after a timeless moment, light began to brighten around him in a glowing, watery haze.

"…He's coming around…"

A voice that sounded like his mother's startled Nick. He looked up. His eyes could barely make out one, then two, then three dark, figures leaning over him. After licking his lips, Nick tried to speak, but his mouth was too dry to form any words. He tried to raise his hand but found that he couldn't move it. When he tried to shift his body, he realized that he was strapped down. He could feel hard metal restraints digging into his wrists, ankles, chest, and hips.

...Mom...?

Nick thought the word, but there was no way he could say it. Even so, he sensed her response to him.

"I'm right here," his mother said.

Her voice was low and soothing. Nick saw one of the dark shapes lean closer to him.

"Our opinion all along is that this has been a serious error in judgment on your part."

This was a man's voice, which Nick didn't recognize.

The steadily brightening light in the room stung Nick's eyes, but he forced himself to look up at the shapes that surrounded him. The more his vision cleared, the stronger the current of fear winding up inside him became until he realized—

They aren't human!

Nick could see that all three of them had huge, rounded, neckless lumps where their heads should have been. When Nick felt something touch his arm, he looked down and caught a glimpse of what looked like a thick, dark tentacle, sliding over his hand.

...Mom...?

"I'm right here beside you, darling."

The pressure on his hand increased. Nick would have pulled his hand away if he could have.

"I'll tell you this," said a male voice. "It's a good thing we implanted the micro-camera into his optic nerve. I can't imagine what would have happened if he and the other had found this chamber without our knowing it."

"We would have found out about it eventually," his mother said.

"Yes, but consider the damage that might have occurred in the meantime."

While this conversation was going on, Nick was concentrating hard, trying to make his vision clearer. Behind the dark silhouettes, he could see bright stainless steel walls, and shelves loaded with what looked like an assortment of strange medical equipment.

"May I give him the injection now? Please?" his mother asked.

It frightened Nick to think that he was going to be given a shot. But even more than that, it scared him to hear such tension in his mother's voice.

Who—or what—are these guys? Nick wondered as he tugged at the restraints on his arms. *Are they the same men who were at the house this morning?...And what do they want?...What are they trying to do to me?*

"No," one of the men said sharply. "The injections will no longer be permitted."

"But...but he enjoys his human form," his mother said, pleading but already sounding defeated.

Human form? Nick thought. He wanted to cry out but couldn't make a sound. *What do you mean, Mom? What's happening to me?*

"And what about the other one, his friend?" his mother asked softly.

Nick heard a watery gasp that sounded like deep laughter.

"We'll deal with him in due time," one of the men in black said. "But for now, we insist that you not give your offspring the injection. It's time for him to change back to his original shape so he can see himself—for the first time—as he *really* is."

Nick struggled hard against the straps that pinned him to the stainless steel table, but he knew that it was useless. His eyes were beginning to adjust to the bright light that reflected off the walls behind the three figures. As his vision cleared, he saw—not human faces at all, but huge monstrous faces. Wide, unblinking, golden eyes above wide, lipless splits in green, wart-covered flesh.

"I—I'm sorry, honey," one of the creatures said.

It was his mother's voice, coming from the huge, ugly toadlike creature that was leaning over him. She—or it—reached out and touched him gently on the side of the face with a soft, wet tentacle.

"But they *are* right," his mother said, her tentacle caressing his face.

Numb terror struck Nick when he looked down at the strap pinning his hand to the table and saw—not a human hand at all, but a long, dark, tapered tentacle!

"Oh, Nicky. Your father and I probably should have told you who you really are a long time ago."

Nick Hansen tried to scream, but it seemed his vocal chords were gone. The only sound that came from his throat was a strangled, watery gasp.

Heidi: I've always been asked if I wanted to be a writer when I grow up, like my mom. I never once said yes. In fact, I've tried every other occupation: probation officer, bartender, private investigator, etc. Some jobs were more interesting than others. Well, I'm all grown up now, twenty-eight to be exact, and it turns out I am a writer. Who knew…well, besides my mom? Writing "Daffodils" together presented a basic problem: I live in Florida, and my mom lives in Massachusetts. Technology made this collaboration possible. I would write a section and fax it to Massachusetts. Then she would edit it and call me with the revisions. Although this was time-consuming, it was also a lot of fun and a great excuse to make too many long-distance calls.

Jane: From the time she was little, Heidi was a storyteller. But she never wanted to be a writer because, as she once said to me, "It's too much like hard work!" However, when the opportunity came to write this story, I didn't call my sons, both of whom I have done books with—Adam, a musician, has done the musical arrangements for seven books with me; Jason, a photographer, has illustrated three of my books. I called Heidi. She said: "I'd love to do it." And by the next morning I had the opening pages of "Daffodils" on my fax machine. She'd send me raw pages, and I'd edit—smooth them; add tension here or there. But basically the story is Heidi's. Now we're at work on a second story, and hope to try a book together. Look out publishing world—here we come!

DAFFODILS

by Jane Yolen and Heidi Elisabet Yolen Stemple

A year after Grandpa Frank died, Grandma Bea announced that she was selling her big house in New York and moving closer to her family. She stayed with us for two months while my mom showed her place after place in our town.

Each night she would come home and say to me, "No character, Jess. Those houses have no character."

I didn't say, but I wasn't sure how a house could have character. I just knew she would buy one of the pretty little new homes that were popping up like weeds. My best friend Megan lived in one. It had carpeting in every room and windows on the ceiling so you could lie on the floor and see the sky. Those new homes were better than our old house, which has cold wood floors and creaky stairs. Megan's house was always warmer in the winter, and in the summer she had air conditioning.

One night at the dinner table, Grandma Bea cleared her throat and asked, "What about the house on Elm Hill, the one with the overgrown lawn? Now, that house has character."

My mother looked up from cutting my little brother's chicken and rolled her eyes, but she didn't say anything.

I knew what house she meant. No one had lived there since I

was little, and I'm ten now, so that's a very long time. When I asked Grandma why she wanted to move into a haunted house, she said, "Jess, I'm not afraid of a ghost or two. In fact, they'll keep me company now that your grandpa's gone. Ghosts are far more interesting than cats will ever be, and they hardly ever have fleas."

Three weeks later, Grandma Bea moved out of our guest room and into the old house on the hill. I was in school when Grandma Bea moved, but that Friday night we went to dinner at her new home. I wasn't sure I wanted to go. After all, there were ghosts there. Everyone said so. But I pretended to be brave—I couldn't let my little brother see that I was scared.

The grass had been cut short and the house painted a new white with gray-blue shutters. It didn't look quite as haunted as it had before, but I still took a deep breath before I entered the front door.

No ghosts bothered us during dinner, which I considered a good sign. I decided not to push my luck and ask about them. After dinner, we left. I wasn't the only one who sighed with relief. When we got in the car, Mom said, "It wasn't as bad as I'd feared."

After a couple months of Friday dinners at Grandma Bea's, I had all but forgotten about the ghost stories. Spring was here, and Grandma Bea had been busy planting flowers on either side of the walk. So when school let out for the summer and she asked if I'd like to spend the week with her in the house on the hill, I agreed. I was even excited about the idea.

Grandma Bea let me stay up an extra half-hour, and then she

tucked me into bed in the yellow bedroom she had made especially for me. Though she knew green was my favorite color, she told me that the room "practically cried out to be done in yellow."

I woke up in the morning to the smell of fresh cut flowers. When I opened my eyes, I saw a small crystal vase with yellow daffodils on the bedside table. The clothes that I had discarded the night before were neatly tucked in the hamper, and new ones were folded on the chair in the corner. The yellow eyelet curtains had been pulled open with yellow lace ribbons, and the sun was streaming in. It made for a cheery morning, and I bounded out of bed and ran downstairs to find Grandma Bea gardening in the yard.

"Thanks for the daffodils," I said as I kissed her on the cheek.

"Oh, Jess, I haven't been able to grow any daffodils here. They seem to die the minute I plant them. It's rather odd. It must have been Mimi."

"Who's Mimi?" I asked as I plucked a weed.

"Well, honey, Mimi's my ghost."

"Ghost?" I asked, but in a whisper.

"A *good* ghost."

I always know when Grandma Bea is done talking, and she was done now. I didn't ask any more questions. And to tell the truth, by the light of day ghosts didn't seem particularly real. Or scary. Besides, who could possibly be afraid of a ghost who brings you flowers in the morning and folds your clothes? I began wondering if this Mimi would clean my room and do the dishes as well.

It was only later, at lunch, that I finally asked about her. Grandma Bea told me that when she had moved in, she began discovering that plates she had left dirty were mysteriously clean the next morning; that windows left closed at night were somehow wide open upon her waking; and that fresh flowers were always left in her bedroom. "But always flowers from the garden, never daffodils. That is very odd indeed."

I decided to trust Grandma Bea's faith in the goodness of the ghost she named Mimi "because she *feels* like a Mimi." I didn't even think about being scared. But that night after being tucked in and left in the moonlit yellow bedroom, I was no longer sure. There seemed to be too many shadows around. Or not enough. I struggled to keep my eyes open, afraid that if I closed them something bad would happen.

But nothing happened.

I guess at some point I finally drifted off, because I awoke with a start late in the night. A crashing sound came from the attic. I pulled the yellow patchwork quilt up to my chin and squinted to try to focus through the sleep in my eyes. Something was moving ever so slightly in the room. In the pale moonlight I could barely make out a figure in the corner rocking chair. It was a woman, much thinner than Grandma Bea. She was wearing a powder blue nightgown, and under her ivory-colored head scarf several unruly blond curls poked out.

I was scared, but felt oddly safe. When I opened my mouth to speak, the woman put her finger to her lips. My eyes became heavy again, and as they closed I heard a faint lullaby sung in a soft but steady voice.

The next moment—or so it seemed—I awoke in a sun-bathed

room to the smell of daffodils. Shaking my head to clear it of the ghost dream, I eased out of bed and grabbed the sundress that lay folded on the rocker. It was then that I saw the ivory-colored scarf draped over the arm of the chair, almost daring me to reach for it. When my hand touched it, I knew the dream was real. I had seen Mimi. She had sung me back to sleep and left me her scarf. I tied it around my waist.

I found Grandma Bea in the kitchen making tea. "That's a lovely scarf, little one," she said "Antique linen. Very nice."

"Mimi left it for me last night," I said. "When I woke up because of a noise in the attic."

"I hear noises from the attic all the time. Probably mice and squirrels. Haven't gotten up there yet," she said, with more than a bit of curiosity in her voice. "You game?"

I guess it was the safe feeling Mimi gave me that made me say yes, but that disappeared the minute we set foot on the rickety old attic stairs. If Grandma Bea felt the same, she didn't say, but I saw her stop and shiver in front of me.

It was dark in the attic, and more than once I jumped from the noise of a loose floorboard. I let out a little screech when I walked into a spider web. And I could have sworn something alive scampered across my sandaled foot.

When I looked around, Grandma Bea was in the corner on her knees in front of a dusty old trunk. She opened the lid and peered in. "It's too dark up here. Let's bring it downstairs, Jess."

I was quite happy to do anything that involved leaving the attic;

it was giving me the creeps. I rushed to Grandma Bea's side and squatted to lift half of the trunk.

We were walking awkwardly toward the staircase, each of us holding an end of the trunk, when we heard an odd thumping noise on the steps. I dropped my half of the trunk on my right foot and cried out. The thumping stopped halfway down the stairs, then started again, ending only when the door at the bottom slammed.

"The wind, sweetie," Grandma Bea said, but she didn't use her usual voice. She sounded hesitant, unsure. I wanted to leave the attic immediately, so I picked up the trunk again and practically pulled Grandma Bea to the stairs. With the door closed, it was almost pitch-dark on the steps, but we managed to get down them, our feet making the same noise as the that weird thumping.

Not until I felt for the doorknob in the dark, found it, turned it, and pushed open the door did I realize that I had been holding my breath. I let it out in a loud *whoosh* as we set the trunk on the ground. Then, after a moment's rest, we lifted the trunk again and managed to carry it down the flight of less noisy stairs to the sitting room. There, I opened it while Grandma Bea fetched iced tea from the kitchen.

On top of the trunk, there were three old dresses just my size— well, maybe a little big. I was slipping a frilly yellow one over my head when Grandma Bea came into the room. She laughed and knelt by the trunk. Throwing me a bonnet that matched the dress, she reached in again, pulling out a handful of yellowed newspaper articles.

"'Town Wife Brutally Slain,'" Grandma Bea read aloud. Then she stopped abruptly, but her eyes spoke for her.

"What Grandma Bea, what?"

"'*Mimi* Foster, wife of Kyle Foster, was found dead in their home at 755 Elm Street, Hatfield, this morning. She had been brutally beaten by an unknown assailant, according to authorities who had to track down Mr. Foster to his mother's home in Whately. Their daughter, Miranda, age eleven years, who was in the house during the attack, has refused to speak a word. She has been taken to her aunt's house'—" Grandma stopped reading aloud and looked up. "Well, it goes on from there."

"When did this happen?" I asked.

"The paper is dated June fourth, 1916. Let's see…that was seventy-eight, no, seventy-nine years ago. There are more articles…" Her voice drifted off as she began to look at the rest of the paper.

Still in the yellow dress, I rushed over to the trunk and dug my hand in past the other dresses. I felt around until my hand hit something hard. I grabbed it and lifted it out of the trunk. A book. It was dusty, so I blew on it, and promptly sneezed. Gold letters showed faintly under the remaining dust—DIARY, it read. I looked up at Grandma Bea, but she was still concentrating on the articles. I opened the diary and read silently.

This is the diary of Miranda Hane Foster
Private Property

I turned to a page in the middle and continued reading.

Dear Diary,

It's late and I can't sleep. Daddy and Mama are fighting downstairs. I hid my head under the pillow, but it did no good. I could muffle their voices, but not the dishes crashing into the walls. Please don't let him hurt her again. Last time we couldn't go anywhere for weeks until the purple bruise on Mama's cheek faded. She said that he doesn't mean it. But she tells me to stay away from him too.

Now, I may be only ten, but I know about these things. I have a friend in school. He lives all the time with his grandparents because his mother ran away from his father when he broke her arm.

I turned to the last page with writing on it.

Dear Diary,

Daddy came into my room tonight when I was asleep. He shook me awake and started yelling, but I couldn't understand him. Mama, who had fallen asleep in the corner chair, jumped on his back and started hitting him. I hid under the bed and closed my eyes tight. When they finally left the room, there was only one set of footsteps on the stairs. I haven't moved. I'm writing this from under my bed. Everything has been quiet since the door slammed. Too quiet.

That was the last thing written. I read it to Grandma Bea. She looked up from the articles and pulled her reading glasses down on her nose.

"From the articles, it sounds as if the police thought Mr. Kyle Foster did it," said Grandma Bea when I had finished reading. "But they never had any proof. Is that diary entry dated?"

I looked at the top of the page. "It sure is: Friday, June third. No year."

Grandma Bea got a curious look in her eye. "Well, little one, are you ready to go to the library? It seems that we may just solve a murder today."

Once at the library, we were informed by a helpful librarian that the information involving the town history was kept upstairs in the Historical Society and was watched over by Mrs. Keppler, who wouldn't be in until two o'clock. Since it was only ten till noon, Grandma Bea recommended we return home for lunch and come back in the afternoon.

On the short drive home, clouds began rolling in. The beautiful day was about to run into rain. By the time we got to the house, the sky was an eerie shade of gray, and the rain had begun. We ran up the walk and were barely inside when a fierce wind began to howl.

"The windows!" yelled Grandma Bea. "Run up to your room and shut yours. I'll get the sitting room."

As I climbed the stairs, the howling got louder and louder, an inhuman wail. I flung open the door and ran to the window. The curtains had broken free from their ribbons and were whipping about in the wind. The room was damp and darker than it should have been at midday, even with the storm. And oddly, the sound of the howling wind seemed to come from behind me.

A chill ran up my spine as I turned to face the noise. In the dimming room, I saw Mimi crouched on the floor, her arms shielding her head. A large bearded man stood above her, his head tilted back, mouth open. No words came out of his mouth, just the sounds of the wind, shrill and cold. Mimi's shoulders shook and her hair seemed matted, not the color of straw this time, but much, much darker.

Effortlessly, the man reached down and picked her up, throwing her over his shoulder roughly and starting toward the door. The sound of that awful wind stopped abruptly, as if cut off by a knife. I must have gasped or made some other sound, because he turned toward me and seemed to smile, but with his mouth, not his eyes. Then he was gone, and light flooded back into the room.

I left the window open and ran down the stairs grabbing Grandma Bea's arm to drag her along with me.

"The library," I whispered. "Hurry!"

After hearing our story, the librarian decided it was a good idea to call Mrs. Keppler in early. Whether she believed us or not, making the phone call seemed better than having two hysterical patrons waiting at her desk for an hour. When Mrs. Keppler arrived, she led us upstairs and sat us down. We told our story once again. Her eyes seemed to brighten. We had her complete attention. When we were finished, it was her turn to tell what she knew.

Clearing her throat, she took a deep breath and began. "In 1916, after Mrs. Foster's murder, the police repeatedly questioned her husband. They were quite sure he had killed his wife. But they didn't have the sophisticated equipment we do now, so it was impossible to prove his guilt. Mrs. Foster's mother swore that he was at her place all night.

"Everyone was pretty sure the little girl, Miranda, had seen everything. The problem was that she never spoke a word after they pulled her from underneath her bed. Not one word from that day on.

"Foster remained in the house until he died in 1958, in his seventies. When I say *remained* in the house, I mean it. He did not come out. Groceries were delivered. The yard became overgrown, and he boarded up the windows. People say that he spent most of his time in the attic, where, incidentally, he died of old age. The groceries piling up on the porch were what clued in the police that he was dead.

"The family immediately put the house on the market. It took a number of years to sell, but in the 1960s people were moving into our town, looking for fixer-uppers. Even those first buyers, though they had the best of intentions, didn't stay. No one stuck around here long enough to explain why they were going. But we knew."

She shook her head. "That house was once one of the prettiest in the town. In fact, Mrs. Foster had made it quite a showcase. Around the turn of the century, a roving photographer took pictures of the houses in Hatfield and their occupants. The Historical Society has them all."

She stood and went to an antique filing cabinet. She retrieved a black-and-white photograph, which she handed to Grandma Bea.

I leaned in to look at the picture. It was unmistakably Mimi with her blond curls. She had her arms around a child, with the same golden curls, who stood in front of her. Both Mimi and the girl looked solemn and a little sad. Next to them was the man that I had seen in my yellow room, with the same smile showing only in his mouth, not his eyes. Like a snake. Behind them was a garden filled with flowers, and the house.

"Look, Jess," Grandma Bea said, her finger on the picture. "Daffodils."

Mrs. Keppler made a *tsk* with her tongue. "The house doesn't look like that anymore," she said. "Though you've made a good start on it. And," she added, "Miranda Foster doesn't look much like that anymore either."

"Miranda?" I said.

"Is she still alive?" Grandma Bea asked.

"Oh, yes," Mrs. Keppler said. "And she's still mute, too."

"Can we meet her?" I asked.

"She might like that," Mrs. Keppler answered. The look she exchanged with Grandma Bea was heavy with meaning. When she turned back to me, she said, "Miranda Foster is in a nursing home. Why don't you tell her about the diary. It might help her to know that it's been found. After all, there is no statute of limitations on murder."

We found the Whately nursing home with no problems and were greeted by a friendly nurse.

"You want to see Miss Foster?" she asked. "No problem. We all love her. She is the sweetest little old lady. But she's mute, you know. Hasn't spoken a word since she was a child."

She escorted us to the garden, where Miranda Foster was sitting surrounded by spring flowers. She wore a light yellow sweater and her legs were covered with a pale yellow lap blanket. Her hair was no longer golden, but pure white. Mrs. Keppler was right. Miranda didn't look like her picture anymore.

I left Grandma Bea talking to the nurse, crossed the garden, and sat on the bench next to Miss Foster in her wheelchair. I explained that my grandmother had bought her old house and made me a room in yellow where hers used to be. She looked at me solemnly, her expression looking a lot like that of the child in the photograph. I told her the story of her mother's singing me back to sleep from the rocking chair.

"And I saw *him*." I told her. "Carrying your mother over his shoulder. His mouth smiled, but not his eyes."

She stared at me and opened her mouth as if to answer, but no words came out. Little tears formed at the corners of her eyes.

We sat there in silence for a little while, smelling the flowers. I felt her put her hand on mine. When I looked up, she was staring at me once more. She lifted her free hand and motioned for me to come closer. I leaned in, my ear close enough to feel her breath.

Although the words were very faint, they were clear and direct. "I…saw…him…too…Tell them my daddy did it."

With those words, she fell silent again. We sat there a bit longer, until Grandma Bea came and gathered me up to leave. I kissed Miss

Foster on the cheek and whispered in her ear, "I'll tell them." As I walked out holding Grandma Bea's hand, I turned to see Miss Foster sitting with her eyes closed.

In the car, I took the photograph out of Grandma Bea's purse. Mimi and her daughter didn't look quite so sad. They weren't exactly smiling, but their eyes seemed happier. Almost peaceful. And in the background, the black-and-white daffodils had a faint glow of gold.

ABOUT THE GREAT WRITERS

❖

RAMSEY CAMPBELL is perhaps the most highly regarded ghost-story writer in the world. He is the award-winning author of numerous short stories and horror novels, including *The Parasite, Incarnate*, and *Obsession*. He lives with his wife and two children in England.

MATTHEW J. COSTELLO has authored many horror novels. He is the writer of the best-selling CD-ROM title *The Seventh Guest,* and is also a contributor to cable's Science Fiction Channel. He resides in New York State with his wife and three children.

RICK HAUTALA is the best-selling author of many horror novels, including *Night Stone, Little Brothers, Twilight Time,* and *Shades of Night*. He resides in Maine with his wife and three sons.

JOHN JAKES wrote fantasy, horror, and science fiction before becoming famous for his eight-volume Kent Family Chronicles and his Civil War trilogy, which are among the best-selling historical novels ever published. With over 32 million copies of his books in print, he still contributes stories to the dark fantasy and horror fields. He resides in South Carolina and in Connecticut.

JOE R. LANSDALE is a multiple-award-winning author of horror and suspense. He has written Batman cartoons for television and has also scripted comic books, including *Jonah Hex, Mucho Mojo,* and *The Lone Ranger*. He lives in Texas with his wife and two children.

ELIZABETH MASSIE is the author of several award-winning novels. Her first book, *Sineater,* won the Horror Writers Association Bram Stoker Award for Superior First Novel. She has also written children's books. She resides in Virginia.

ANNE McCAFFREY has authored dozens of best-selling fantasy novels, including the blockbuster series The Dragonriders of Pern®. The winner of both the Hugo and the Nebula awards given by the Science Fiction Writers of America, she has also written many short stories of dark fantasy. She resides in Ireland.

JILL M. MORGAN, who also writes under the pen names of Meg Griffin and Jessica Pierce, is the author of over 22 novels, including *Cage of Shadows*. She writes for adults and children in a variety of genres, including horror, mystery, and suspense. She lives in California with her husband, two sons, and daughter.

MAXINE O'CALLAGHAN has written ten novels in the mystery and horror fields, including *Dark Time*. She also writes the highly praised Delilah West, Private Eye series. She lives in California with her husband.

PETER STRAUB is the best-selling author of many popular horror novels, including *Ghost Story, Shadowland, Floating Dragon, Koko,* and *The Talisman,* which he co-authored with Stephen King. The winner of the World Fantasy Award for Best Novel, the British Fantasy Award, and the August Derleth Award, he lives in New York City with his wife and two children.

MELANIE TEM is a multiple-award-winning writer whose past honors include the British Fantasy Award. Her first novel, *Prodigal,* won the Horror Writers Association Bram Stoker Award for Superior First Novel. She lives in Denver, Colorado, with her husband and four children.

GAHAN WILSON is a horror author as well as a renowned artist. His unique cartoons and creepy creatures have appeared in such diverse publications as *The New Yorker, Omni, Gourmet,* and *Playboy*. He resides in New York State.

F. PAUL WILSON has written a number of best-selling horror and suspense titles, including *Sibs, The Select,* and *The Keep,* which was made into a feature film. A practicing physician, he lives in New Jersey with his wife and family.

JANE YOLEN has authored more than 150 books for children and adults. Her many honors include the World Fantasy Award, the Kerlan Award, the Christopher Award, and the Regina Medal for her contributions to children's literature. Jane Yolen lives with her husband, David Stemple, in western Massachusetts.